Two Plays

And Give Us the Shadows

and

Autumn and Winter

Two Plays

And Give Us the Shadows

and

Autumn and Winter

by

Lars Norén

Translated by

Marita Lindholm Gochman

Chaucer Press Books
An Imprint of Richard Altschuler & Associates, Inc.

Los Angeles

Distributed by University Press of New England

Two Plays: And Give Us the Shadows and Autumn and Winter by Lars Norén. Copyright © 2013 by Marita Lindholm Gochman. For information contact the publisher, Richard Altschuler & Associates, Inc., at 10390 Wilshire Boulevard, Los Angeles, CA 90024, (494) 279-9118, or richard.altschuler@gmail.com.

Library of Congress Control Number: 2013932737
CIP data for this book are available from the Library of Congress

ISBN-13: 978-1-884092-85-5

Chaucer Press Books is an imprint of
Richard Altschuler & Associates, Inc.

Printed in the United States of America

Distributed by University Press of New England
1 Court Street
Lebanon, New Hampshire 03766

Contents

Foreword

PRESENCE. Presence is the only word that comes to mind when I think of Lars—an absolute presence in the present, in the now—both as playwright and stage director.

I have had the privilege of working closely as Lars Norén's producer since 2000. During this period he directed many of his own works as well as plays by other playwrights: Chekhov's "The Seagull," Shakespeare's "Hamlet" and Ibsen's "Little Eyolf." We have collaborated on productions in Sweden as well as in Paris, Berlin, Copenhagen and Oslo.

As a director, Lars is absolutely present while working. His sensitivity and keen ear, and his ability to "take in" the actors during the rehearsal process, is different from any other director I have worked with. He very seldom looks at the script while rehearsing. Instead he asks the actor to speak the words over and over again in order to make sure the text is understood. He will often concentrate on the character that is listening rather than on the one that is speaking. In those moments he reminds me more of a musician or a musical conductor. His productions are known for their rhythms and musicality.

As a playwright, Lars has an extraordinary ear for character-driven dialogue, a deep understanding of "us"—contemporary humans. There is never a word that feels wrong or false, those small, almost insignificant words that say so much. With those words and the small details, he creates a universal recognition of the characters and events in his plays— a recognition that resonates to a wide variety of audiences around the world.

There is a belief among many who have not read or seen a Norén play that he writes "difficult" and complicated plays. On the contrary, his language is always clear and direct and very easily accessible. One doesn't have to "understand." You hear the words and you know—you recognize. He is expressive as well in what's not being said; what's between the lines often speaks as loudly as the spoken words.

Sometimes it seems that a playwright is born for a certain time, a certain place, and for actors of just that time. I believe that's why Lars Norén is here right now. He is truly an actor's playwright, and invariably his text makes the actors give extraordinary performances. His writing is perfectly suited for today's actors. That's why so many want to work with Lars's plays. There exists a mutual love and respect between Lars and the actors, whether they are in France, Germany, Denmark or Sweden.

Even if many of Lars Norén's plays contain darkness and horror, they are never considered heavy. There is lightness in the language and in his way of writing that doesn't weigh audiences down. There is such tenderness and love for the characters in his plays, however horrible their behavior might seem.

And then there is his sense of humor—that constant, ever-present sense of humor, that keen eye and ear for the absurdities within our human condition. Sometimes it's difficult to recognize that the sense of humor is present when the theme or storyline seems so harsh and unrelenting—but then, there it is, a small word, a pause or a full sentence that breaks the horror and brings in the laughter, sometimes as a release, sometimes as pure zaniness.

The sense of humor and ability to laugh at oneself is a constant factor in working with Lars. How we have laughed together and with others over all these years! However heavy the reality of our lives has been, we've still laughed. So through our work and our laughter Lars has become my friend. My very dear friend.

Ulrika Josephsson, 2013
Artistic Director,
Folkteatern Göteborg
Olof Palmes Plats
Sweden

Translator's Introduction

by

Marita Lindholm Gochman

"How DO you translate a play?" I hear that question often. I don't really know. I think the process of translating a play is as diverse as the people giving it a shot. I can talk about my own way of working, which is very much like how an actor or a director would approach a play. I start by reading the play several times. I make notes to myself about the different characters, the exact moment in time—the when, the where, and the why. Yes, everything that I want to have available in my brain before beginning to write. I try my hand at a longhand version. I look quickly at the Swedish script and then I scribble the first thing that comes to mind. I try to absorb the line, not overthink it or the words in it. I write it down the way it hits my senses. After I finish I rarely look back at my longhand version. What it gives me is a first glimpse of something—not an understanding, but a snapshot of a whole—that is very important later on in the process.

Now comes the time to write the first draft of the translation, which becomes a kind of roadmap into finding the play in English. When I sit down at my computer I start fresh. I try to hear the characters' voices; I try to understand their thoughts behind what they are saying. This process is not about "subtext"—that's for the actors to find out—but, instead, it's about finding why the characters are saying what they are saying without saying it. Lars Norén is a master of that: Rarely do his characters say what they are thinking.

I should mention that my first language is Swedish, which means that the third step is the most crucial step for me. I make my dear husband, Len, sit down with me—Len with the English translation and a red pen in hand—while I'm checking the Swedish script, my handwritten notes, and my trusted, old thesaurus close by; and slowly, slowly we go though the play line by line, word for word. It helps a lot that Len is an actor. His questions are always illuminating.

Since Lars Norén is often writing in a kind of "everyman speak" in Swedish, with all its quirky and non-grammatical inconsistencies but with his mastery of it—still a strangely poetic language—you are always faced with the question as to how it should be reflected and interpreted in a big, precise language like English. This conundrum is not about different dialects or a language flavored by where the characters live or originate from but, rather, it is about the way the characters express themselves, in the way the grammatical errors show up and how "slang" is used. The latter allow us to begin to understand the characters in a profound and specific way. This is when the idea of translating words stops being helpful. This is when the characters have to shine through, reveal themselves, because of how they express themselves or are unable to express themselves. This is when an American audience has to be comfortable listening to foreign characters speak and accept what they are saying. Since Len doesn't have any Swedish language lurking in his brain, his reactions to the translated lines become invaluable.

Is what's being expressed in English the same as what's being expressed in Swedish? Is the translation too right on, too clear, too pat? Is it possible to find a more nuanced interpretation of the line? Of course, there is no way that the uniquely Swedish people Lars writes about will ever "pop out" in the powerful way they do on the Swedish stage.

Many years ago I found this quote. I copied it and put it in my file, and I'm sorry to say that I don't know who to give credit to regarding this very perceptive thought about translations: "Think of language as a piece of paper: The 'thought' is the front of the paper and the sound is the back, you cannot cut the paper without touching both sides. In language you can't isolate the sound from the thought or the thought from the sound."

I also have a favorite poem written by Vladimir Nabokov during his time working on the poems by Pushkin.

> What is translation? On a platter
> A poet's pale and glaring head.
> A parrot's screech, a monkey's chatter,
> And profanation of the dead.
> The parasites you were hard on
> Are pardoned if you have your pardon,

O Pushkin, for my stratagem.
I travelled down your secret stem,
And reached the root, and fed upon it;
Then, in a language newly learned,
I grew another stalk and turned
Your stanza, patterned on a sonnet,
Into my honest roadside prose—
All thorn, but cousin to the rose.

Once the cleaned up English version exists, I try to put together a "reading" with actors. Even more preferable is a weeklong workshop with a director and actors. During this process the questions that come up usually lead to different ways of expressing a thought or solving the problems of certain tricky areas. Working with actors usually exposes the gulf between two cultures: What's funny in Sweden can be very sad in America and vice versa—and it is also the time when the translator is wondering if the playwright's "voice" has been completely lost. What did I do? Where is the play—where did it go?

In a small country like Sweden, the need for drama written in a different language than Swedish, in order to keep the demand for theater filled, is the rule. Therefore the process I just described is usually built into the rehearsal process. In America the translated script is often seen as a frozen script. There is no time during the rather short American rehearsal period to fine-tune the script. Also, in Sweden one person always present at early rehearsals is the dramaturge. A dramaturge many times functions as a cultural bridge, or someone who is able to clarify the cultural differences to the director and actors. Fortunately it's becoming more common here in the U.S. to engage dramaturges in the process of creating theater.

About "And Give Us the Shadows" and "Autumn and Winter"

The two plays in this book very much represent the long journey that Lars Norén and I have travelled together in my effort to bring Norén to America.

"And Give Us the Shadows" was sent to me in 1991. I still remember the big package that arrived from the Royal Dramatic Theater in Stockholm, where Lars had his home base at that time, weighing in at several pounds. I think the running time of that version must have been over six hours long. I worked day in and day out in order to have a first draft ready before the big opening in Sweden. Lars invited me to sit in on the final week of rehearsals. I learned so much from observing the actors become the O'Neill family on stage. It should be said that Swedish actors are given a long rehearsal period, sometimes as long as three months. This was a play that really benefited from extensive rehearsals. The cast was superb. Max Von Sydow played the mighty Eugene O'Neill himself. He had absorbed both the grandeur and the tragedy of the American genius. Margaretha Krook played Carlotta, Eugene's third wife; Reine Brynolfsson played Eugene Jr.; and Peter Anderson played Shane, the brother of Oona and half-brother of Eugene Jr. The director of this premiere production was Bjorn Melander. The play received wonderful notices from the Swedish critics. It was still long, but had been cut down to about 4-½ hours by the time it opened. In my translation I followed the cuts that had been made by Lars and Bjorn.

As an aside it should be noted that Eugene O'Neill has always been an important playwright in Sweden in the Ibsen/Strindberg tradition. In 1923 the Royal Dramatic Theater produced "Anna Christie" followed by many other O'Neill productions. After his death in 1953, Karl Ragnar Gierow, then head of the Royal Dramatic Theater, contacted O'Neill's widow Carlotta—supposedly with Dag Hammarskjold as intermediary—to inform her of the theater's interest in any plays as yet unperformed. The Royal Dramatic Theater was given exclusive rights to stage the world premieres of four plays: "Long Day's Journey into Night," "A Touch of the Poet," "Hughie," and "More Stately Mansions." In 1956 "Long Day's Journey into Night" had its world premiere at the Royal Dramatic Theater and is still considered one of the high points in that theater's history.

So much has been written about "And Give Us the Shadows," especially in Sweden. My own understanding and sense of the play is that, at the core, it speaks of a complicated, contemporary family, a family we can all relate to. It is both ancient Greek drama and modern situation comedy. It is dark and filled with humor; it deals with the most mundane issues as well as the most profound issues of our lives: a husband's illness, a wife worried about what will happen to her after he is gone, children who are rootless and confused, a family dealing with drug abuse and alcoholism.

When I came back from Sweden in the spring of 1991, I told George White, founder of the O'Neill Theater Center in Waterford, Ct., about this remarkable play, and on the spot he invited the whole cast to the Playwright's Conference in Waterford that very summer.

What followed was a string of readings, two years of work with a producer in London, and innumerable discussions of how to proceed with "And Give Us the Shadows." I finally moved on to other Norén plays, and this play ended up on a shelf in my office. It wasn't until 2011 that I took a good look at the play again, and with the blessing of Lars and the help of Moni Yakim, director and teacher at the Juilliard Drama Department, I sat down and made serious cuts in order to make it a viable play for the American stage. This is the version contained in this book.

"Autumn and Winter" has a similar story. It opened at the Royal Dramatic Theater in Stockholm in 1992 to great reviews. Once again a superb cast was assembled, with Anita Bjork as the mother and Lill Terselius as the troubled daughter. (Anita had portrayed the unforgettable Miss Julie in the 1951 Swedish film version of the Strindberg play.) I was there for the opening, and again I had a first draft of the translation in my briefcase. A few months later I went back to Stockholm, this time with my husband, and Len read the play to Lars. It seemed to us that this play would very likely have a smooth journey toward an American production.

The great people, especially my friend Niclas Nagler, at the now defunct Circle Repertory Company organized a reading of "Autumn and Winter" shortly after Len and I came back from Sweden. The reaction to the play was overwhelmingly positive, and then—nothing. There have been other readings after the first one. I especially remember one time, at the Rattlestick Theater in Greenwich Village—in conjunction with the production of "War," also by Lars Norén—the wonderful actor David Margulis—who read the role of the father—saying "Autumn and Winter" was the female version of "Long Day's Journey into Night." That was a lovely thing for me to hear. I will always treasure David's reaction to the play.

In 2010 I decided along with several of my friends—including the director Eleanor Reissa, the actress Bo Corre, and the producer Niclas Nagler—to option "Autumn and Winter" from Lars. We set out to cut the play to a length desirable by the American theater, with Lars's blessing, of course, and our goal was to bring it to the American stage. This book contains the shortened version of the play, which we have worked on in workshops and fine-tuned through a number of readings for theater audiences. The play is still set in Sweden and the characters are Swedish, but most references to Sweden have been removed. My feeling is that the people in the play are easily recognizable in American society. It's a play about generational issues and family dynamics that are universal. The idea that an unspoken but forever life-changing event between husband and wife will have profound consequences for the children later on is not new; but it is always important and worth discussing. As in "And Give Us the Shadows, "Autumn and Winter" has no heroes, no good versus evil—just ordinary people trying to live the best lives they are capable of living.

"And Give Us the Shadows" and "Autumn and Winter" were written during a period (1985 through 1992) when Lars Norén was exploring the Swedish upper middle class. By the mid '90s he seems to have left that area of interest forever. Instead he turned his spotlight on a whole spectrum of difficult societal subjects, such as criminality, the Swedish prison system, the Swedish mental health system, war, displacement due to war, immigration, neo-Nazism, and the faltering safety net for the poorest in Sweden as well as in the rest of the world. He has often been called "Sweden's social conscience."

Beginnings: On First Meeting and Translating Plays by Lars Norén

I went to meet Sweden's "new August Strindberg" (to quote Swedish theater critics at the time) at his apartment in Stockholm. The year was 1982. I rang the doorbell, and the door was opened by a young man who just pointed to a leather couch and disappeared in the direction of a crying baby in need of attention. That was my introduction to Lars Norén. I guess he thought I knew what he looked like, but I didn't.

Looking around, I saw that I was in an old, beautiful, high-ceilinged, very dark row of rooms, where Norén lived with his partner and their brand new baby girl, Nelly. This space I entered was one I would recognize over the years in the stage directions for many of his early plays. It was very sparsely furnished, but whatever was in it was expensive and exquisite. Usually stated in the stage directions—as in the apartment I was in—there would be an Italian leather couch; perhaps a big piece of art; a bike; stacks of books and international magazines on the floor; and some black and white photographs on the mantel of the fireplace.

I was surprised when he came back (after a very long time) and sat down next to me and asked if I had seen his play at the Royal Dramatic Theater titled "Night Is Mother to the Day." The play had caused a sensation in Sweden and Lars had become a household name overnight. I was pleased to report that I had seen the production the night before our meeting, and also pleased that I could honestly say it had been a most memorable experience. I had been transported through the writing and the stagecraft into a different universe, a universe that was to become quite familiar to me over the years—the Norén universe: a universe inhabited by strong, flawed, egotistical, loveable, often cruel and narcissistic characters, very much like most of us; people who love, hate, question why they exist, but fight ferociously for recognition and their own little place on this earth.

Lars loves the characters he creates. There are no heroes, no winners, just ordinary people being exposed, with their weaknesses, fantasies, hopes and dreams—dreams that rarely come true. With his extraordinary sense of humor and his compassion for the underdog, he creates drama out of the most mundane situations, such as illness, madness and boredom. He is always on the side of the child whether the child is young or old.

My mission in Sweden was to secure the American rights to "Night Is Mother to the Day." Lars was mildly interested at the time, but at least we met face to face. Eventually we got the rights problems sorted out and the play opened on a cold March night in 1984 at Yale Repertory Theater in New Haven, Ct. The production was directed by Goran Graffman (the same director as in Sweden) and the play had been translated by Harry G. Carlson. I was very pleased with the production. The wonderful American actors had formed a strong family feeling, and the black humor had not been lost in translation. The Yale students wrote about the play in glowing terms. Mel Gussow, however, the *New York Times* critic at the time, wrote a devastatingly bad review, which made every effort of moving the play to New York an impossibility.

After the debacle in New Haven, I was convinced that Lars no longer would want anything to do with me. I had heard that the Swedish press had jumped all over the news of the bad review, and that Lars felt burned by it. Then one October day in 1985 a very big package arrived by mail. It contained a working script of "The Last Supper" (with over 600 pages), a play that was being prepared for a production at the Royal Dramatic Theater in Stockholm and subsequently opened in 1986, with a running time of six hours, starring Lena Olin and Erland Josephsson. The play was set in real time. Since the action in the play starts around eleven p.m., the audiences were invited into the theater at that time. They were seated in comfortable easy chairs and advised to bring food and drinks. This production became a "must see" cult phenomenon in Stockholm. Years later I met with Erland Josephsson in New York, and his recollections of that production were vivid. He said that it had been one of the most exhilarating and most exhausting acting challenges of his long stage career at the Royal Dramatic Theater, but that at the end of the play audiences and actors were bonded in a way he'd never experienced before or after.

The task of translating this huge play was enormous but exciting. At that time there weren't any computers readily available (at least not in my house), so the typewriter was my only friend. I started out by numbering every line in the play and the translation. That gave me a starting point when it came to finding my way in the vast script as far as cuts that were being made. It took a long time to bring "The Last Supper" in front of an American audience, but in 1989 we did a reading at St. Peter's Church in New York, which was very well received, and a few years later there was a production of the play at La Mama in New York.

That was the beginning of my working relationship, as a translator, with Lars. What followed was a string of Norén plays. I think I have worked on as many as twenty-five plays from different periods of Norén's vast body of work.

My husband Len and I would travel to Sweden to meet with Lars, and Len would read the translations aloud to him, in order to give him a sense of what the American cadences sounded like. As a teenager, Lars was a lover of the black and white Hollywood movies of the forties; therefore his ear for English is excellent. He will invariably question words or sentences that we, ourselves, have questions about.

We have been lucky to spend wonderful moments, both in Sweden and in New York, with Lars and his family over a long period of time. The man that I met in the old Stockholm apartment many years ago has, of course, changed over the years—less hair for sure—but the essence of the man is the same. He is still the passionate "teller of truth" that he always was. He is still the playwright who tries to penetrate more deeply into our human condition, to go where drama has never gone before, with a profound understanding of—as was commonly said in Europe of Lars Norén's work—"le comedie inhumaine."

And Give Us the Shadows

Characters

Eugene: Eugene O'Neill

Carlotta: Eugene's Wife

Eugene Jr.: A Son

Shane: A Son

Saki: The Japanese Butler

ACT ONE

SCENE ONE

Marblehead, Mass., Oct 16, 1949. While the Japanese butler, Saki, quietly clears the breakfast dishes from the table in the dining room, Eugene and Carlotta walk into the living room, where heavy curtains are pulled shut covering all the windows facing the sea, which leaves the room in semi-darkness.

CARLOTTA

You need to eat, Gene. One cup of coffee isn't enough . . .

EUGENE

Isn't Fred coming today?

(Eugene picks up The New York Times *and a stack of telegrams off the table. He opens the paper but doesn't read it.)*

CARLOTTA

Fred never comes on a Sunday, today is Sunday, Gene. I had to take bromide last night because you kept me up again. I didn't sleep at all. Aren't you going to open your telegrams? Gene?

EUGENE

Why?

CARLOTTA

Why? Maybe they would cheer you up a bit. Who knows? There isn't one word about you in *The New York Times* today. (*pause*) Elia Kazan has written something about the Belasco Theater. . . . I really would like to see *A Streetcar Named Desire*. I could spend a few days in New York . . . meet some friends . . . talk to some lawyer . . . about Bennett Cerf and his little weasel of an editor, Saxe Commins. Anyway, when you die I'll move back to New York. Gene, dear, are you going to stay silent the whole day?

(Saki enters, stands quietly and waits, until she finally notices him.)

CARLOTTA

Yes, Saki?

SAKI

Ma'am, I'm finished now. Is there anything else you'd want me to do?

CARLOTTA

No thanks, Saki dear. . . . Relax a bit until the good-for-nothings arrive. Oh, there is one thing . . . Estaban (*Carlotta's beloved toy monkey*) . . . upstairs. Could you please fetch him for me?

(*Saki bows and leaves.*)

CARLOTTA

He's just like an American, only more refined. Gene, try looking a little more cheerful, otherwise we'll lose him too. (*walks over to Eugene and grabs his tie*)

EUGENE

Don't.

CARLOTTA

Your tie, darling, the knot looks awful. (*unknots and redoes his tie*) Lift your chin. My only company is a Japanese butler and Doris, our simple minded cook! (*pause*) At times I would like nothing better than to relinquish all my responsibilities and feel like an ordinary woman. Do you understand what I mean?

EUGENE

Yes.

CARLOTTA

There. Now it looks good. (*Eugene tries to pick up a pack of cigarettes from the table. Instead, he pushes the lamp down, the shade comes off but the lamp doesn't break. Carlotta walks over, picks up the lamp and puts the shade back on.*) I've sacrificed my life just to take care of the house and manage our business. Be your secretary . . . and nurse . . . and lover of sorts. . . . (*pause*) (*Eugene holds his left wrist to keep it from shaking.*) I was a young, innocent woman when I met you. . . . You called and asked if you could come up for a cup of tea. You had four cups and you sat there looking like a brooding Hamlet. Then you looked at your watch and said, "Oh my God, I have to go." And you ran away. Why did you want to see me?

EUGENE
I don't know. . . . I wish I knew.

CARLOTTA
I fell in love with you. I've travelled near and far with you, new places, shabby hotels. . . . You were used to all that.

EUGENE
I was born in some goddamn hotel room.

CARLOTTA
To me it represented everything that was cheap and tawdry.

EUGENE
And I'll probably die in some goddamn cheap and tawdry hotel room.

CARLOTTA
Everybody said that the romance with that dark haired actress would end after three weeks and you'd return to Agnes and the children. (*Saki comes into the room holding the stuffed monkey. She walks up to him and takes it.*) Thank you, Saki.

(*Saki leaves.*)

EUGENE
I've never had a chance to put down roots.

CARLOTTA
You and your damn roots.

EUGENE
(*laughs*) Even the Barrett House, where I was born, has been torn down.

CARLOTTA
He's the only boy I ever had. (*smiles at Estaban, the stuffed monkey, and hugs him*)

EUGENE
Near Times Square . . .

CARLOTTA

Gene dear, are you going to change your will or not?

EUGENE

Let's not talk about money this early in the day.

CARLOTTA

Will you or won't you? I believe I have the right to some compensation for everything I've done for you.

EUGENE

(*reaches out for the cigarettes*) Would you be kind enough to get me a cigarette?

CARLOTTA

Yes, if you promise to rewrite your will. Don't scrunch your brow. You look so incredibly old. You had a mother and a father. You lived in a big home with a big lawn. . . .

EUGENE

That wasn't a home, that was a hellhole! You don't know what you're talking about!

CARLOTTA

I've heard the same story for twenty years. I've typed that play three times. I know what it's about! (*She gives him the cigarette.*) I wonder what they would say . . . all your "loving" friends, who think I'm Lady Macbeth keeping you locked up out here. . . . If only they knew how dependent and utterly helpless you are . . . without me! If I hadn't saved your damn letters, I wouldn't have any proof at all!

EUGENE

What letters?

CARLOTTA

Your lyrical love letters to me, when we were apart from each other!

EUGENE

I guess everyone writes a love letter now and then . . . even I.

CARLOTTA

I guess so.

EUGENE

Where do you keep them?

CARLOTTA

The letters? Where you can't find them.

EUGENE

I want to rip them up.

CARLOTTA

You can't even rip up a cigarette.

EUGENE

I don't want anyone to find them if I were to die.

CARLOTTA

If you were to die? What do you mean by "if"? (*laughs*) No one will
FIND them, because I'll have them published as soon as you're gone.

EUGENE

Those are my letters, my words — my feelings . . .

CARLOTTA

Now they're mine, you gave them to me, you wrote them to me. Gene,
you've smeared your love all over me!

EUGENE

You're horrible.

CARLOTTA

Thank you. You wrote them to your beloved wife. I am your beloved
wife!

EUGENE

You've taken too much bromide.

CARLOTTA

I hope you die soon.

EUGENE

So do I.

CARLOTTA

Ah, to be free, to rid myself of this damn life with you. (*She walks over to the fireplace and takes down a picture of the two of them, both smiling tenderly, leaning against an enormous oak tree in some forest in France.*) My God, I look like I was happy. Young and hopeful. . . . Gene, you must understand. We'll have to tend to your business before it's too late.

EUGENE

I don't give a damn about it.

CARLOTTA

There are problems we have to deal with whether we want to or not, because of the two sons you have. And before that agent-editor of yours, Saxe Commins, and all the other grave-robbers steal everything.

EUGENE

There's not a damn thing to steal. I'm forgotten, gone.

CARLOTTA

Yes, but sooner or later they'll discover you again. What do you think they'll say after they've read *Long Day's Journey into Night*?

EUGENE

They never will! You swore to me with your hand on the bible!

CARLOTTA

Of course I did. I'll simply have to starve to death.

EUGENE

I don't want to talk about it anymore.

CARLOTTA

We've nothing left to live on. I've used up all my savings so that you would have a real home! What are we going to do?

EUGENE

I'm going to talk to Saxe . . .

CARLOTTA

When?

EUGENE

Soon . . . as soon as I feel a little stronger.

CARLOTTA

My God, you've got to do something, before you die. (*pause*) It makes me sick to think about how the people who exploit you are going to be your literary beneficiaries. And your children . . . You wouldn't want them to look after your masterpieces.

EUGENE

What does it matter when we're gone?

CARLOTTA

You might be gone, but I'm not. (*looks at Estaban*) It's wonderful having someone around who's always smiling. (*pause*) One o'clock! I told them we're eating at one . . . not sooner nor later. (*pause*) Kidney.

EUGENE

I've eaten so much kidney lately, I'm beginning to feel like piss.

CARLOTTA

You must tell them once and for all that we can't give them any more money. (*pause*) Also, try to talk some sense into your son.

EUGENE

Which one?

CARLOTTA

The one it's still possible to talk to. The communist. I dislike everything about that man. He never calls me Carlotta. He only says, "How's the diehard Tory? (*pause*) Wasn't it enough that you gave them a third of the income from "Mourning Becomes Electra?" (*long pause*) Saki, Saki!

SAKI

(*Saki comes in.*) Ma'am.

CARLOTTA

(*smiling*) I just wanted to know if Doris had remembered to put the meat in the oven.

SAKI

It's already in the oven.

CARLOTTA

Thank you. I don't know what I would do without you, my dear Saki. (*Saki bows and leaves.*) I don't understand how they could place people like Saki in those prison camps. He's as good an American as you or I. (*pause*) If you'd only go for a walk during the day you wouldn't have to spend half the night listening to that jungle music. My God . . . if Blemie wasn't dead, you could be taking him for a walk every day.

EUGENE

Yes.

CARLOTTA

How could we have left him in California? I hated it there. The only thing of value in all of California is Blemie's grave.

EUGENE

That's true all right.

CARLOTTA

Finally something we agree on! Wonderful! He was the only one of our children who never disappointed us.

EUGENE

I think about him every day. I even dream about him. Last night I dreamt I had the *Electra* script in my lap. I knew I had never written as well before . . . so, I threw it away, but Blemie ran after the papers and brought them back to me.

CARLOTTA

He thought he was a retriever. . . . He was so full of life.

EUGENE

And loyalty and love.

CARLOTTA

You never wrote anything as beautiful as your epithet to Blemie.

EUGENE

He stayed by my feet the whole day while I worked. Had I not managed to write that play I would have given up. I had abandoned my children. I spent more than nine hundred days writing that damn play.

CARLOTTA

Our first play.

EUGENE

I wanted to destroy the kind of theater Papa strutted around in. Now I'm not so sure it isn't a melodrama just like *The Count of Monte Cristo.*

CARLOTTA

Don't start that again. Open your telegrams instead.

EUGENE

Still, Dad was so damn proud of me. (*pause*) Why is it so dark everywhere! Is it because you don't want me to see how old looking you are?

CARLOTTA

No, so I don't have to look at you! You know damn well I can't take light anymore! That's your fault! My eyes are destroyed. . . . My God, when I think how I worked on *Electra*, how I sat bent over a typewriter while the years dwindled away. "Mourning Becomes Electra" is MY play. Lavinia and I . . . the same fate has befallen us. (*smiles*) One thing is clear—that damn play does not belong to Saxe Commins! It should be mine!

EUGENE

Now, let's be friends.

CARLOTTA

Before they get here?

EUGENE

Before we die. (*laughs*)

CARLOTTA

You're immortal, you'll never die . . . unfortunately. I can't be your friend. I'm a normal woman with very normal needs! I need a man—not a legend. (*pause*) I'd better go to the kitchen to make sure we can feed your senseless prodigal sons. (*But she doesn't leave.*)

EUGENE

I remember that time when you came to visit your friend, Florence Reed, and you left your scarf behind . . . and Florence said she'd be back tomorrow to fetch it since Gene is here.

CARLOTTA

That's a lie! A lie!

EUGENE

I don't think I even noticed you.

CARLOTTA

What an idiotic notion! I really did forget my scarf, but not on purpose. I left things behind everywhere! I couldn't believe that was you, that dark, strange man, who sat alone on the veranda, not saying a word; that you were Eugene O'Neill, who'd written "The Hairy Ape" that I, unfortunately, had been in! It was embarrassing to me. (*smiles*) I remember once when we walked together in the woods. It was terribly hot. As I was taking off my hat, it got stuck on a hairpin. You tried to help me, but you were too nervous, and I took your hand away from my hair. We stood breathlessly still and I was wondering what you'd do to me. Perhaps he's violent, perhaps he's going to leap on me. But oh no—you didn't even kiss me. You just took my hand, like an altar boy, and told me that my eyes were like your mother's.

EUGENE

I didn't know many young women. I had no idea what they were thinking about, what kind of dreams they had.

CARLOTTA

(*laughs*) That was in the twenties and you already looked like Mr. Depression himself. (*pause*) I was so happy when we finally could live openly together, without having to hide from Agnes and the reporters. I was so happy that day in Paris. (*Tears fill her eyes.*)

EUGENE

(*moved*) I was, too . . . Carlotta. (*With tears in his eyes.*) Carlotta.

CARLOTTA

That day in Paris . . . the eighteenth of July, 1929, when we were finally husband and wife.

EUGENE

That was the happiest day of my life, my darling Carlotta. (*Eugene tries to hug her.*) I love you. Don't push me away. Forgive everything I've done, and everything I will do!

CARLOTTA

That day when we both said *"Oui"*. . .

EUGENE

Carlotta, I love you.

CARLOTTA

You don't know how to love.

EUGENE

My love is as deep now as it was then. I know I'm ungrateful. (*tries to kiss her but she turns away*) You don't know what it's like for me!

CARLOTTA

I know what it's like for me!

EUGENE

To want to write, but not being able to . . . I've never had anything else to live for, except my writing, and now that's over.

CARLOTTA

That's really delightful to hear. I don't mean anything? I'm nothing to live for?

EUGENE

Carlotta, you know how much you mean to me. You're the only one I've ever loved.

CARLOTTA

Words, words, words . . . words, words, words.

EUGENE

I'd die if you left me. You're the only true and good thing in my life.

CARLOTTA

If you love me, then why did you give away the rights to Random House? I don't give a damn about "Iceman" or "Strange Interlude," but "Electra" is mine, it's . . . our story. (*pause*) Why didn't you write anything to me on our wedding anniversary this year? I only have nineteen notes, and we've been married twenty years.

EUGENE

You know how hard it is for me to write. It takes me an hour just to write a check.

CARLOTTA

Because you're stingy and selfish.

EUGENE

Stop it now! Stop it!

CARLOTTA

I stopped a long time ago! I'm not asking for much. You've got Parkinson's, but it hasn't killed you yet.

EUGENE

But it inhibits my ability to create! The ideas don't come if my hand doesn't move across the paper.

CARLOTTA

I don't think I've ever seen you happy. I don't think you were happy on the day we were married . . . or that night. (*pause*) My wedding night.

EUGENE

That's enough. Now stop it.

CARLOTTA

A night I'll never forget. We came back to the hotel and you said I'm exhausted, I'm going to bed. You went to your bedroom and I to mine. That was my wedding night. Any man would have given anything to make love to me. That's probably been the hardest thing in my life with you. I never felt that you had any erotic longing for me. I know that Agnes . . .

EUGENE

Now, keep quiet!

CARLOTTA

She didn't have a barrel of fun either. (*laughs*)

EUGENE

Shut up!

CARLOTTA

You just sat there on her bed, the way you do with me, looking at her in the dark . . .

EUGENE

Shut up!

CARLOTTA

You detest women, except when you need them!

EUGENE

You make me want to vomit!

CARLOTTA

You've never given a thought as to what might happen to me when you're gone.

EUGENE

I know exactly what will happen. You'll be moving from one presidential hotel suite to another, one endless shopping spree through Bergdorf Goodman, dinners at Quo Vadis. If I had used all the money I've spent on you to open a chain of whore houses from New York to San Francisco, I'd be a wealthy man today! (*laughs*)

CARLOTTA

What are you saying?

EUGENE

And I would've had a hell of a lot more fun!

CARLOTTA

What are you saying?

EUGENE

I was making fifty to seventy thousand dollars every year, and I have nothing left!

CARLOTTA

I'm going to kill you.

EUGENE

You do that!

CARLOTTA

(*Carlotta picks up a fireplace tool and grabs it with both hands.*) I've had enough. I'm putting an end to this, you goddamned son of a bitch!

EUGENE

Saki! Saki!

CARLOTTA

I'll kill you, I'll kill you!

EUGENE

Saki! Saki! Hurry up!

CARLOTTA

It won't help calling him. He's on my side! He's my servant!

SAKI

(*Saki enters.*) Ma'am, Sir.

CARLOTTA

(*Carlotta lets go of the fireplace tool.*) Saki, I just wanted to ask you to light the fire in here. It's getting cold and damp.

SAKI

Yes, ma'am. (*bows and starts to put some logs in the fireplace*)

CARLOTTA

Please pour me a little scotch when you're done, so that the world takes on a rosy hue again. (*smiles*) I'll wear black for the rest of my life. I look just like Lavinia Mannon in "Mourning Becomes Electra." Did you ever see "Mourning Becomes Electra," Saki?

SAKI

Sorry, ma'am, I did not.

CARLOTTA

No, you're much too young. Alla Nazimova played Lavinia. I should have played her. I was an actress. I was talented. I could've made it big, but then I met Eugene O'Neill. (*pause*) How's Doris doing? It's almost twelve o'clock. (*short pause*) Please go and fetch me the three hatboxes from the coat closet. I want to try them on, to decide which one I'll wear.

(*Saki goes out.*)

EUGENE

I've surrendered everything that most people live for—friends, family, children . . .

CARLOTTA

You never cared about your children!

EUGENE

I surrendered life itself. I saved my soul, but lost the world. (*laughs*) I've existed in a tomb since 1912. That summer of 1912, I was frozen in time.

CARLOTTA

1912, your divorce and your tuberculosis is something I shouldn't have to suffer for. (*laughs*) I'll let you die in that hotel room all by yourself, Gene.

EUGENE

(*after a short pause*) I made millions with "Anna Christie"—and now there's nothing left. Where's all the money I've made? Where is it? (*Eugene looks at his violently shaking hand as Saki is coming back with three hatboxes.*)

CARLOTTA

You've wasted it on your goddamn kids and wives, books and castles and cars. You needed to prove you weren't some little Irishman, the son of a third-class actor. Thank you, Saki.

EUGENE

I should have stayed in Provincetown, in that simple house by the sea.

CARLOTTA

All you want is to be locked up with me in your private hell, but that's not what I want! (*Carlotta walks over to the bar and pours herself another glass of scotch.*) Gene, darling, the reason we're poor is that they aren't doing your plays. No money is coming in. The money is depleted. That's what happens to money, idiot.

EUGENE

(*Eugene holds up his shaking hands.*) You make me shake, you wrinkled old bitch!

CARLOTTA

You should talk about wrinkles! Hah! I'm still beautiful, and there isn't one man who would say no to me, if I wanted him. (*door bell*) You've been impotent for the last ten years; add that to the list of things you can't do anymore. (*Saki enters.*) Saki, darling, please get the door. (*Saki walks into the hall.*) (*speaks in a lower tone of voice*) Gene, I've told Saki to collect all the cartridges he can find. I know you keep the shotgun next to you up there, just waiting to shoot me. . . . (*Laughter is heard, male voices.*) Your sons . . . they are here. The addict and the bum, the royal family from the Province of Tyrone.

SAKI

(*Saki shows Eugene Jr. and Shane in.*) Mr. Eugene and Mr. Shane.

SCENE TWO

(*The same room. Eugene is at one end of the room looking frightened; Carlotta is at the other end, fuming.*)

EUGENE JR.

(*His voice is hoarse and slightly affected. One can hear he is a drinker.*) Hello, dear Carlotta, hello, Father. Well, here we are. Nice to be here. (*Carlotta keeps staring at them.*) Recognize us?

CARLOTTA

All too well.

EUGENE JR.

(*laughs*) And I'd hoped you'd be happy to see us.

CARLOTTA

Hope all you want.

EUGENE JR.

At any rate, nice to be here. (*He takes a few steps towards Eugene.*) How are you, Dad?

EUGENE

I don't know.

EUGENE JR.

Good. Nice to see you. It's been a while. Two years.

CARLOTTA

Can two years go this quickly?

EUGENE JR.

Good, you still have your sense of humor.

CARLOTTA

And my keen intellect.

EUGENE JR.

Right. Congratulations, Dad, and happy birthday.

SHANE

(*Shane stays in the shadow of Eugene Jr.*) That's right. Congratulations, Dad, I hope you're well. It's nice to see you. Nice to see you. We came by train. Yes, very nice to be here. It's very nice here.

CARLOTTA

Why are you here so early? Nothing is ready yet.

EUGENE JR.

It's not that early, really. This place is much farther away than we thought. Beyond the horizon. The end of the road. The last station. After this there's only ocean. From the desert of New York to "the vasty deep" of Marblehead.

CARLOTTA

You've gotten fat.

EUGENE JR.

So?

CARLOTTA

Fat-ter.

EUGENE JR.

You old hawkeye, you. (*laughs*) Well, we were just standing out there, wondering, if you were at home or not.

SHANE

Yes.

EUGENE JR.

It looked so deserted we thought you might have found some safe haven to avoid the onslaught.

CARLOTTA

What onslaught?

EUGENE JR.

From people who want to pay tribute to America's greatest playwright, the Sophocles of our uncultured time.

SHANE

Journalists. *The Herald Tribune*. *The New York Times*.

EUGENE JR.

We were almost sure we wouldn't be let in. (*laughs*) I'm joking.
(*to Carlotta*) You look good.

CARLOTTA

I wish I felt good. (*to Shane*) You look ten years older than you are.

SHANE

Well, I am. . . . I've had some problems with my teeth.

EUGENE JR.

(*Eugene Jr. puts his arm around Carlotta. She doesn't like it.*) So, how are you, you diehard old Tory?

CARLOTTA

(*Carlotta moves away.*) Your breath could kill me.

EUGENE

So, how are you two doing?

EUGENE JR.

Fine, thank you, fine.

EUGENE

Are you working?

EUGENE JR.

Work, what's that? (*laughs loudly*) (*to Shane*) Do you know what that is?

SHANE

No, I don't, I've forgotten. (*also laughing*) Sorry.

CARLOTTA

I've never understood your Irish sense of humor.

EUGENE JR.

(*Eugene Jr. puts his arm awkwardly around Eugene.*) "On'y sixtyone, daday! My old stepdad lived to be ninety. . . . "Licker can't kill the O'Neills!"

EUGENE

That's fine. That's good. (*Eugene pulls away.*)

EUGENE JR.

America's only play of destiny. It's a great play, Dad. Hell, it's the greatest play ever written in this country. Even Euripides would have been proud of "Mourning Becomes Electra." And, oh, yes . . . (*Eugene Jr. takes a bouquet of roses and a bottle of red wine out of a shopping bag and gives them to Carlotta.*) I almost forgot. Please, dear Carlotta.

EUGENE

How nice. Look at that, they bought flowers.

CARLOTTA

Thank you. Charming . . . how European.

EUGENE

Very thoughtful.

EUGENE JR.

The roses are from Times Square, and you are as beautiful as a rose-velt! Ha, ha.

CARLOTTA

I would appreciate if you didn't talk about that communist in my home.

EUGENE JR.

A communist? Our dear President Roosevelt, may he rest in peace.

CARLOTTA

We can thank Roosevelt for having spread the seeds of communism in this country.

EUGENE

You must know by now that Carlotta is even more reactionary than the British Royal Family.

CARLOTTA

And proud of it. (*to Eugene*) You haven't spoken to Oona since she married the communist Jew. Don't you know she hopped on a plane with suitcases filled with Charlie Chaplin's money and tucked it away in a Swiss bank.

EUGENE

That's not why I haven't spoken to her. Let's not talk about that now.

SHANE

I liked what Roosevelt said during the war. He was like some kind of . . . great uncle.

CARLOTTA

I don't care what you think. He allowed narcotics into this country to weaken the people and make them unable to defend themselves when Stalin comes here with his butchers. We should have helped Hitler to destroy the Russians instead of getting together with them. I hear there are at least fifty Russian spies working in the State Department. We should have dropped the bomb on Moscow—not on Japan.

EUGENE

Let's not talk politics now.

EUGENE JR.

You're right. It's pointless. It's wonderful to see you, Dad. How do you feel? Do you like it up here?

CARLOTTA

Great writers never LIKE anything. They go through life suffering while making life miserable for others. (*Eugene Jr. laughs.*) Well, you can laugh.

EUGENE JR.

What else is there to do.

CARLOTTA

Why don't you take off your hat? Saki, dear . . .

SAKI

Ma'am.

EUGENE JR.

(*He gives his hat to Saki.*) Oh, sorry.

SAKI

(*Saki takes the hat.*) Sir.

CARLOTTA

. . . and the flowers, please.

(*Saki bows and leaves.*)

EUGENE JR.

You look better, much better, than when you were in New York. (*pause*) It must be the sea and everything. One can hear the sounds of the waves. It would make me nervous, but you like the sea. (*laughs*) I'll get nervous if I can't have a drink soon.

CARLOTTA

It's too early, even for you.

EUGENE JR.

It's never too early. Shane thought we'd gone to the wrong place but the cabdriver said it always looks this desolate. He even knew who you were. He said he's seen "Mourning Becomes Electra" on tour in Boston. He still remembers it. He told us how he'd never forget how Lavinia went into the house and closed the door—and how he got "goosebumps" all over.

EUGENE

That's right. At the Colonial Theater . . . he remembered that?

EUGENE JR.

He said he'd never forget it.

SHANE

Goosebumps.

EUGENE

That's a long time ago, 1931.

EUGENE JR.

The same year I graduated Yale and received the Winthrop Award for my outstanding knowledge of Greek and Latin poetry. If only the world had continued speaking Latin and Greek, everything would have gone my way, Dad. (*laughs*) You were so proud. Do you remember, Dad?

EUGENE

I vaguely remember something like that.

EUGENE JR.

You told me you were so proud of me. (*laughs*) He's much too educated for me, you said.

CARLOTTA

Oh, we remember. We remember you had to ask permission from Yale to marry that poor girl you had gotten pregnant. (*laughs*)

EUGENE JR.

My God, Dad was expelled from Princeton because of drinking. He went to the theater and visited brothels instead of going to school. . . . But that's all forgotten now.

CARLOTTA

I wish I could forget.

EUGENE JR.

(*laughs*) Anyway, the cab driver asked us to congratulate you on your birthday. It seems there's an article in today's *Boston Post* about you, Dad. Something about the prodigal son coming home.

EUGENE

Home? Where?

CARLOTTA

You don't even know what a home is.

EUGENE JR.

Here somewhere. Boston . . . Connecticut . . . New England.

EUGENE

I have no home. I don't belong anywhere, least of all in New England.

EUGENE JR.

Same with me.

CARLOTTA

You'll find a home . . . somewhere in hell.

EUGENE JR.

(*laughs*) That sounded like a line out of one of your plays, Dad.

CARLOTTA

Most of them he got from me—the good ones.

EUGENE

After all these years, that's what she's become.

EUGENE JR.

(*laughs again*) Anyway, these New England folks, they seem proud to have you here again.

CARLOTTA

Oh yes, they think he's so nice and pleasant, while I'm treated like Lavinia.

EUGENE JR.

Oh, my God, I brought you a gift. It's just a book. President Truman says hello, too. (*laughs*)

SHANE

Not Roosevelt. (*laughs*)

EUGENE

Thank you. Very nice, very nice. There was an air of lynching in the theater when the *Electra* tour came to Boston. They were as upset as if I had defecated in church.

CARLOTTA

Gene, please!

EUGENE

They treated me like dirt. They thought I was ridiculing them. *The Boston Herald* wrote "Why does Mr. O'Neill find such pleasure in presenting the people of New England as degenerates?" How could I be so ungrateful . . . here, where they showed such hospitality by opening up their homes, inviting the Irish working class directly off the streets into their drawing rooms. We were the underclass, treated like servants— worse than Negroes because Father was an actor! Don't think that those fancy ladies invited my poor mother to any of their sacred tea parties. I'll never forgive them for the way they treated her. If she'd had some form of social life, she wouldn't have felt so lost. She might even have conquered her addiction.

CARLOTTA

Why didn't you do something to help her?

EUGENE

I did what I could.

CARLOTTA

Yes, you went out drinking with your brother. (*Saki enters holding the vase of flowers.*) Put them on the dining room table, please. Shane, you don't talk very much, do you. It's actually quite pleasant.

EUGENE JR.

Shane.

SHANE

Sorry? What did you say?

CARLOTTA

How are your children?

SHANE

Fine . . . they send their regards. They have colds.

CARLOTTA

How many children do you have now?

EUGENE JR.

Ruth also sends her regards. She's anxious to see you again, Dad.

CARLOTTA

Ruth . . . Ruth . . . Ruth.

SHANE

Yes . . . they send their regards.

EUGENE

Thank you. How are they?

SHANE

Fine . . . they're fine . . . just that they have colds.

CARLOTTA

Well, you have to take care of them.

EUGENE JR.

The gift, Shane! Your present!

SHANE

Oh yes, something I bought. Just something small.

CARLOTTA

How nice. We like presents. (*laughs*) What would this world be without presents?

SHANE

I don't know. . . . (*Shane searches his pockets and finds a small packet.*) Here it is. It's nothing special.

CARLOTTA

It's the thought that counts.

EUGENE

You shouldn't have. Thank you.

SHANE

It's nothing special. It's a pen. A fountain pen. Well, I thought . . . since you . . .

EUGENE JR.

Since you are a writer.

SHANE

They said it's a very fine pen. It'll last for fifty years if you're careful. (*laughs*) Well, you know what I mean. (*laughs*) Also, Cathy sends her regards. To everybody.

CARLOTTA

What did you say? Speak a little louder.

SHANE

Sorry. (*loudly*) I said that Cathy sends her regards to everybody. She's sorry she couldn't come. We thought it would be too much trouble, and quite expensive too, if the children were to come.

CARLOTTA

We didn't expect any children. We live quite isolated out here.

EUGENE

Yes, that's God's truth.

EUGENE JR.

(*short pause*) I've got some news. Ruth, the girl I've been with for years . . . well, we're going to get married.

SHANE

You and Ruth? You're getting married?

EUGENE JR.

Yes, why not?

CARLOTTA

When did you start to appreciate matrimony?

EUGENE JR.

Probably when I got divorced. (*laughs*) Anyway, we've lived together for so long that we might as well.

SHANE

A wedding would be nice. Are we invited?

CARLOTTA

What do you think you can offer her?

EUGENE JR.

I think it's time for a stable life before I turn forty in a few months. (*laughs*) I've always had the strange feeling that I'll be gone before I'm forty. (*pause*) I have some plans. Maybe I'll try to get into showbiz somehow. I've talked to a couple of producers I know. I . . . if not, I can always go back to teaching Latin or prosodical elements in English poetry.

EUGENE

You're as unrealistic as ever.

EUGENE JR.

We'll go on living in Ruth's apartment. .Maybe you'll come down to New York soon?

EUGENE

I'll never go back to New York again. I've always hated that city and the people in it.

EUGENE JR.

But wouldn't it be fun to go to the theater and see some of the new plays? "Death of a Salesman, " "A Streetcar Named Desire."

EUGENE

I haven't been to the theater in fifteen years . . . except for the godawful rehearsals for "The Iceman Cometh."

EUGENE JR.

That's what I've always said. Dad never goes to the theater. He has the theater within him. August Strindberg felt the same way.

SHANE

I never go to the theater either.

EUGENE

Strindberg knew what he was talking about. The theater is a whorehouse.

CARLOTTA

That explains why you liked it so much.

EUGENE JR.

(*starts to laugh*) I was just reminded of that story about the "Iceman." The husband is relaxing in the bedroom on the second floor waiting for the iceman to deliver the ice; now and then he calls down to his wife, "Did the iceman come yet?" "No," she says, but his breathing is getting heavier. (*laughs*)

(*Eugene laughs too. Carlotta makes a grimace, but even she laughs eventually. Shane looks at them and smiles.*)

CARLOTTA

So, the children send their regards to the old grandparents.

EUGENE JR.

Dad, do come down to New York some week-end. We could go to a baseball game or a boxing match.

EUGENE

I hate New York.

EUGENE JR.

We could go downtown and listen to Billie Holiday at the Village Vanguard.

CARLOTTA

If only I had the strength to go to New York for a weekend and meet some real people; if I only had a girlfriend I could talk to, someone to laugh with.

EUGENE

You have your Virgin Mary.

CARLOTTA

I have nothing. I've been alone since the day I met you!

EUGENE JR.

Well, I'm getting hungry.

EUGENE

You mean thirsty.

CARLOTTA

You'll soon get some food. So . . . you're getting married again? What do your other three wives think about that?

EUGENE JR.

Were there that many? I hope they'll realize what they've been missing.

CARLOTTA

Was that supposed to be funny?

EUGENE JR.

No, I've lost my sense of humor.

CARLOTTA

Haven't you ever thought about returning to Yale? How are you going to provide for a wife?

EUGENE JR.

I've moved down to the Village with Ruth. To your old haunts, Dad. I love the Village life, but I guess you have to live here in order to work, right? You've always said the sea was your home.

CARLOTTA

When we moved here he said it reminded him of his summers in New London. . . . Later I learned that those summers were the worst of his life.

EUGENE JR.

It's strange how things repeat themselves.

SHANE

Yes. (*pause*) Where's the bathroom?

CARLOTTA

Upstairs, but don't touch anything.

EUGENE JR.

I've always had the feeling that . . . that in some way I'm like Uncle Jamie. (*pause*) People thought he was the one who would become famous. Not Dad. Have you visited New London Yet?

EUGENE

No.

CARLOTTA

What would we visit there? That ghostly, dilapidated, old house?

SHANE

I have to . . .

CARLOTTA

For God's sake, GO!

SHANE

Thank you. Excuse me. I'm sorry. (*Shane leaves.*)

EUGENE JR.

It would be interesting to see the place where you grew up, you and Jamie.

EUGENE

What's there to see? Just a house. A tired old house.

CARLOTTA

A tired old house, like any other old house.

EUGENE

We only used it during summers, but it was our home. The only one who took care of it was Papa.

CARLOTTA

(*to Eugene Jr.*) If he uses drugs in this house I'll throw him out.

EUGENE JR.

Why would he do that?

CARLOTTA

Because he's a drug addict.

EUGENE JR.

He said he stopped. He's given his word of honor.

CARLOTTA

Word of honor? This family could start a business selling broken promises. Once an addict always an addict. They never tell the truth . . . right, Gene? How many times did your mother give her solemn oath?

EUGENE

Don't start.

CARLOTTA

It's terrible he has to go through this again.

EUGENE

I don't care anymore.

CARLOTTA

He's your son, for God's sake!

EUGENE

I can't do anything. I never could.

CARLOTTA

I can't either.

(*She listens and hears Shane coming down the stairs. Everyone looks at Shane.*)

SHANE

What's the matter?

EUGENE JR.

Nothing.

SHANE

I'm just a little tired.

CARLOTTA

In 1931, when we had just returned from Europe, we paid a quick visit to New London.

SHANE

You had a Cadillac then.

EUGENE

A Cadillac?

SHANE

A big, white Cadillac.

EUGENE

Sounds like we were millionaires, but it was a secondhand Cadillac.

SHANE

Once we rode in it, Oona and I, when we were in New York visiting. (to Eugene Jr.) Weren't you with us?

EUGENE JR.

No. (*laughs*) It wasn't the best time for me to see Dad. I thought he was angry with me.

CARLOTTA

He was! The way you were ruining your career and marrying that little trollop.

SHANE

You had a real chauffeur, a chauffeur in a uniform.

EUGENE JR.

I could understand that Dad didn't have any great desire to attend my wedding.

EUGENE

However stingy Papa was we still had the first Packard in all of Connecticut. He got it for mother's sake, for her enjoyment.

EUGENE JR.

Dad has also been married three times. I didn't even know that Dad was my . . . dad. (*laughs*) I'd think that living with my mother must not have been all that inspiring.

CARLOTTA

How can you say that about your mother? (*pause*) After all those horrible stories I'd heard about Gene's mother, I thought he'd rather not see that house again. (*laughs*) Well, I was stunned when I finally saw that adorable little birdcage. But when we stood there looking at it, Gene said we shouldn't have come. Then we never talked about it again ,until he started to write about it.

EUGENE JR.

(*after a while*) But here, it's nice here, isn't it?

SHANE

Yes.

EUGENE JR.

I can't think of living anywhere but New York.

SHANE

Everyone ends up in New York, sooner or later.

EUGENE

What do you do? How do you make a living?

EUGENE JR.

(*laughs*) I get by.

EUGENE

I guess you're doing the same thing you've done since you left Yale— just bumming around.

EUGENE JR.

I've been very busy . . . doing different things.

EUGENE

You were a shining star at Yale. And you threw it all away.

EUGENE JR.

There was a war, Dad. I didn't think lecturing about Virgil was appropriate while people were being killed.

CARLOTTA

Please, don't blame the war!

EUGENE

Unlike Shane, you always had a good head for studies. He never could concentrate long enough on anything.

SHANE

I enlisted in the Navy after Pearl Harbor.

EUGENE JR.

I tried, but they didn't want me!

SHANE

The best thing I ever did.

EUGENE

I've done everything I could for the two of you, and you know it! (*to Shane*) I often tried to steer you in the right direction. I made sure you went to the best and most expensive prep school in the country. What did you do? After a couple of weeks you got homesick and wrote to Agnes, and she went straight up there and brought you back home.

SHANE

(*quietly*) I wanted to go back to Bermuda. I liked Bermuda. That was the only place I ever liked. It was paradise.

EUGENE

Well, one has to grow up sometime; one can't remain in paradise forever.

CARLOTTA

Agnes did everything to make us suffer. She delayed signing the divorce papers because she was hoping that Gene and I would get tired of each other.

SHANE

I had a good time in Bermuda. I didn't like that prep school. I didn't make any friends No one was visiting me. Gaga was the only one who cared about me.

EUGENE

Gaga was the one who destroyed everything. She took over the family the day she arrived. If you didn't get your way you always knew that Gaga would give in to you. You think you've had it hard—you have no idea of what I had to go through. Everybody said I abandoned my family for Carlotta's sake. I tell you, there wasn't one moment I didn't miss you. I was ready to get on the next ship back to America, but I had to stay in Europe.

CARLOTTA

What a lovely thing to say.

SHANE

I dunno . . . (*laughs a little*) I guess I got the idea that everybody was deserting me. Gaga was the only one there for me.

EUGENE

I'm not saying anything about Gaga. I had a nurse myself I loved when I was a child. (*to Eugene Jr.*) You had a nice wife, a good apartment. You could've gone as far as you wanted, become anything you wanted. Now that there's no damn Depression out there, even a "good-for-nothing" could find a job. What do you do about it? You just drift along.

SHANE

Dad, don't start on Gene now.

EUGENE JR.

That's not fair, Dad, I've had plenty of jobs, but I'm trying to find my own path. I also have a touch of poet in me. I'll find something that suits me.

EUGENE

Become an alcoholic—that suits you.

EUGENE JR.

Dad, I've had some interesting job offers I'm considering. It's true.

EUGENE

Well, that's good.

EUGENE JR.

You haven't heard it, of course, but I've worked as a radio announcer in Hartford a few times.

EUGENE

As a what?

EUGENE JR.

A radio announcer, doing commercials and introducing programs. Many say I sound like Orson Welles. You know, the guy who did *The War of the Worlds* ten years ago. (*laughs*) They say I could be a new Orson Welles.

EUGENE

You can become an elevator operator if you want. What the hell is that—sounding like someone else?

CARLOTTA

(*to Estaban*) Have you ever heard anything as silly as that?

SHANE

Are you going to be an impersonator?

(*Eugene Jr. walks over to the table with liquor bottles, doesn't take a drink, and goes back to his chair.*)

EUGENE

Go ahead . . . have a drink.

EUGENE JR.

A little Scotch won't kill me.

CARLOTTA

(*stands up*) I have to go to the kitchen and talk to Doris about our lunch. Don't you get drunk now, or am I wasting my breath?

EUGENE JR.

Dad . . . Dad, rumors have it that you weren't exactly a choirboy either, you and Uncle Jamie. You two hung around the sleaziest hangouts on Broadway. You even wrote about it. You drank and gambled on horses, and you had no real job either.

EUGENE

You don't know what you're talking about. The times were different. Everything was different. I didn't get an education. The street and the sea were my university. Then I became ill and I thought I didn't have long to live. I didn't give a damn what kind of life I led! I grew up in bars and second rate hotels! I didn't know how to get away from it, but you seem to like it, down there in the muck, and you're obviously trying to pull

Shane down with you. If it isn't liquor it's something else. Neither one of you has any real backbone! (*to Eugene Jr.*) If I only felt that you'd really tried. I'm not talking about Shane now, he's a dreamer, always was. Gene, you're almost forty. When I was forty I already had a body of work behind me. And stop talking about Jamie as if he was some kind of romantic hero from the past. You don't know anything about him.

EUGENE JR.
No, Dad, I know I don't know anything.

EUGENE
You don't know anything! That's what's wrong with you! Jamie wasn't what you think. He was a sick and unhappy human being. The difference between him and others I've known, who are waiting for the big break, was that he was too intelligent to deceive himself. He destroyed his life with booze and whores knowing full well what he was doing. If that's what you want, you're heading in the right direction. But for God's sake, don't think there are any similarities between you and Jamie. Jesus, there wasn't one single day of happiness in his life. Only a goddamn idiot would try to emulate him.

EUGENE JR.
Please calm down, Dad. I'm not trying to be like Uncle Jamie.

EUGENE
You've studied Greek. They have a saying, "Know thyself." . . . Know thyself . . . that shouldn't take too long.

EUGENE JR.
I . . . well . . . forget it . . .

EUGENE
Forget everything! That's your philosophy.

EUGENE JR.
I just happened to run into one of your old producers and I asked him if he could find something for me, and . . .

EUGENE
Find something!

EUGENE JR.

Yes, anything. A job in radio or TV . . . or maybe, well, who knows, maybe as an actor.

CARLOTTA

You? An actor? My word.

EUGENE JR.

Something. Some minor role. One has to start someplace.

CARLOTTA

A very minor role in that case.

EUGENE JR.

I'm even taking voice lessons. I know you have to work very hard.

EUGENE

How the hell do you think you could become an actor just like that? If you had any talent for acting it would've been evident a long time ago. We haven't seen it, have we?

EUGENE JR.

No, you're probably right.

EUGENE

I know I'm right.

EUGENE JR.

Well, I might as well kill myself.

EUGENE

I guess that's always a solution.

SAKI

(*Saki enters and waits for Carlotta to notice him.*) Ma'am . . .

EUGENE JR.

OK, Dad, I'm not capable of anything.

CARLOTTA

Yes, Saki.

SAKI

There's a telephone call for Mr. O'Neill, ma'am.

CARLOTTA

Who is it?

SAKI

A journalist, ma'am.

CARLOTTA

How strange. (*She walks over to the telephone.*)

EUGENE

Even way back then, when Papa was performing, you had to have a certain talent to be in the theater, at least you had to have the looks for the stage.

EUGENE JR.

It's not like it used to be. One doesn't have to look like Clark Gable.

CARLOTTA

This is Mrs. O'Neill. Hello. (*pause*) No, Mr. O'Neill doesn't give any interviews. (*pause*) No, he has nothing to say to anyone. (*pause*) He's feeling very well. (*pause*) Why don't you listen to me? (*pause*) We have nothing to say about Mr. Chaplin. Good bye! (*Carlotta comes back.*) They interrogate us as if we were criminals!

SHANE

They even used to call me to ask about you, Dad, but they don't anymore.

EUGENE JR.

It hasn't been easy having a father named Eugene O'Neill.

CARLOTTA

If anyone has taken advantage of the name O'Neill, it's you!

EUGENE

Choose any name you want if it isn't good enough for you.

CARLOTTA

Where would you be if your name wasn't O'Neill?

EUGENE JR.

Yes, but . . . on the other hand you're always considered some kind of an appendage. They try to find traces of Dad in me. I've tried to stake out my own life, but sometimes it feels like there's no point in trying. You've always seemed so far away, beyond reach. I couldn't ever see you as an ordinary father . . . I didn't even know you were my father. (*laughs*) I thought that man playing baseball with me was my dad. When I learned the truth, I felt a deep hole, a void I've been trying to fill ever since.

CARLOTTA

If you don't like the name O'Neill, there's nothing preventing you from taking your mother's name, Jenkins. That's a good American name. Eugene Jenkins.

EUGENE JR.

Yes, why not.

CARLOTTA

For God's sake Shane, can't you sit still? You keep bouncing up and down like a Jack-in-the-box!

SHANE

Sorry. I can't really sit still any more.

CARLOTTA

Why?

SHANE

It's too hot in here.

EUGENE JR.

I think so too. Can't we open a window? We need some air.

CARLOTTA

If I get cold my arthritis gets worse. (*sees Saki*) Saki, is lunch ready?

SAKI

I was just about to tell you that lunch is served.

CARLOTTA

Finally.

SHANE

I'm not very hungry.

EUGENE JR.

Perhaps Shane and I should go for a little walk after lunch. Some fresh ocean air would be good for him.

CARLOTTA

Saki, please open the window while we eat. (*Carlotta stops Eugene Jr. and Shane as Eugene goes first into the dining room.*) (*in a low voice*) Not a word about Oona. Don't ever mention her name in this house. (*to Shane*) He had great hopes for you; he was so proud when you joined the Navy.

EUGENE JR.

We won't talk about the past. (*bows for Carlotta*) How does an old, diehard Tory feel about having a communist for dinner?

CARLOTTA

What do you think?

SHANE

I'm just going upstairs to wash up.

ACT TWO

SCENE ONE

(*The same room an hour later. Carlotta, who seems happy and satisfied, is the first one to come out from the dining room. The others follow. Shane seems even more tense than before and moves about with uncertainty. Eugene Jr. has had enough to drink to feel free to be himself. Mr. O'Neill looks dour and resolute.*)

CARLOTTA

We haven't been to the Savoy for years. I never see anyone but Gene, and I'm tired of looking at you, darling. (*sits down*) Please sit down. Saki and Doris really are the only living souls we socialize with. I'm really a very shy person. On stage I was different though. . . . (*laughs*) There I could hide behind roles that were different from me. (*pause*) But then I met Gene, married him and now I'm here. (*short pause*) And then there's Fred, our Italian barber, who comes here and cares for Gene's mustache. He treats me like an exquisite diva—constantly complimenting me—and is politely indiscreet. One needs a little indiscretion living out here in the wilderness. (*Carlotta notices Saki.*) Saki . . . Saki . . . dear Saki, come here. (*Saki comes in.*) I think I'd like a little after-dinner drink. Would anyone else like a drink?

EUGENE JR.

Yes, please.

CARLOTTA

Excellent. I like people who drink now and then. There are only three important things in this world: eat, drink and make love.

EUGENE JR.

(*laughs*) I agree.

CARLOTTA

In that order, but I haven't done much of the last one for a long time. (*to Shane*) Shane dear, what's wrong with you?

SHANE

I'm cold, I'm sick, I have cholera.

(*Saki gives Carlotta a glass of whiskey.*)

CARLOTTA

Thank you, darling. Shane, is it true that you tried to commit suicide a while back?

EUGENE JR.

(*short laugh*) Shane? Where did you hear that? Shane? Never.

CARLOTTA

That's what we heard. He turned on the gas in the kitchen. How idiotic.

SAKI

(*bows, in a low voice*) Anything else, ma'am?

CARLOTTA

No thanks. I'll call you if there's anything else.

SHANE

Did Cathy tell you that?

CARLOTTA

I don't remember who told us. Eugene was destroyed for weeks. Just imagine, having a son trying to take his own life. What if you had succeeded? What if it had been in the papers?

SHANE

That's not what happened.

CARLOTTA

You are crazy.

EUGENE JR.

Now he's here, young and healthy. Let's just be happy that Cathy came home in time.

CARLOTTA

What do you mean by that? Doesn't she usually come home in time?

EUGENE JR.

How the hell would I know when Cathy gets home! I hardly ever see them.

CARLOTTA

Watch your tone, young man.

EUGENE JR.

Yes, yes, I'm sorry. (*drinks*) Well, cheers . . . to the good life.

CARLOTTA

To what has been.

EUGENE JR.

(*to Eugene*) Cheers for sobriety, as Uncle Jamie used to say. (*drinks*)

CARLOTTA

Gene doesn't drink. No matter what they say, he really stopped twenty years ago.

EUGENE JR.

I know. (*laughs*) If only half the rumors of Dad's early life were true, you'd be "perfectly pickled" in a jar, Dad.

CARLOTTA

(*to Eugene*) Try looking a little happier, dear, the kids are here. Smile, dear.

EUGENE JR.

Yes, cheer up, Dad.

CARLOTTA

I'll tell you this, your father is a very strange creature.

EUGENE JR.

(*starts to sing*) "Grab your coat and get your hat. Leave your worries on the doorstep." . . . Do you remember? (*sings again*) "Just direct your feet to the sunny side of the street." (*Carlotta sings along.*) "Don't you hear the pitter pat." (*He repeats the last verse, holding the last note for a long time.*) I love it, it's wonderful, it's America!

CARLOTTA

From the "gadawful" thirties.

EUGENE JR.

We shaped this century.

CARLOTTA

That's a song by Dorothy Fields

EUGENE JR.

And that we ruined, too!

CARLOTTA

(*takes Gene's hand*) In the thirties, my Gene never did anything but work. It's terrible to spread rumors about him being an alcoholic. We've been married for twenty years and I've only seen him drunk perhaps three or four times. I asked him how he got the strength to stop. (*looks at Gene*) You said you had reached a point where you had to decide if you were going to be a genius or an alcoholic. (*short pause*) Maybe it would've been better if we'd had more boozing and fewer plays. (*laughs*) I really wanted to marry this man to give him security. Does that sound ridiculous? Yes, it sounds ridiculous.

EUGENE

No, my darling . . .

EUGENE JR.

No, no, not at all.

SHANE

(*whistles "On the Sunny Side of the Street"*)

EUGENE

I wouldn't be alive today if it weren't for you. I wouldn't have had the strength to live. Carlotta, my beloved. I have you to thank for everything.

CARLOTTA

I think so too.

(*Eugene Jr. stands up and walks over to the table with the bottles.*)

SHANE

Couldn't we sing a little more?

CARLOTTA

There's no reason to sing.

EUGENE

I really don't care what people say, as long as I have you.

CARLOTTA

You should care. People, they are the ones going to the theater. We survive on what people think. Why don't you write a play about me? I've often wondered about that.

EUGENE JR.

Or about me.

SHANE

Not about me, please. (*Shane is about to go upstairs.*)

EUGENE

Where are you going?

SHANE

I was just going . . . up there . . . to the bathroom.

EUGENE

Again?

SHANE

I was just going to wash up.

EUGENE

Why? You aren't dirty.

EUGENE JR.

Relax Shane, have a drink. A little whiskey will do you good.

EUGENE

Don't lure Shane to drink. You ought to watch your own drinking.

EUGENE JR.

I can handle it.

EUGENE

You're an alcoholic.

EUGENE JR.

I've never missed a day of work because of drinking.

CARLOTTA

You've never had any work to miss.

EUGENE

(*to Eugene Jr.*) Don't drag your brother down when he's trying to get up.
You've always had the worst influence on him.

SHANE

No, Dad. Dad . . . Gene never tried to . . . .

EUGENE JR.

I haven't seen Shane for six months! This is really the first time I've seen him since he was admitted. I've never had anything to do with drugs. That's something he found all by himself. I've enough trouble looking after myself. I take a drink to relax, that's all.

CARLOTTA

Let's talk about something else. Tell us about New York . . . what's happening on Broadway?

(*Eugene walks over to the window to get away from them. He bumps into Shane, who's going upstairs. Shane stops and smiles.*)

EUGENE

What's wrong with you?

SHANE

Nothing's wrong.

EUGENE

Why the hell didn't you stay a seaman on a ship, instead of crawling around amongst the dregs!

SHANE

But I . . .

EUGENE

Did you hear what I said?

EUGENE JR.

As Dr. Freud said, there's a reason for everything.

SHANE

Yes, I'm sorry, I shouldn't . . .

EUGENE

Don't you care about anything? Why the hell did you start with that shit?

SHANE

I don't know, there was a war and . . .

EUGENE

Don't blame the blasted war! Neither the war nor the Senate is at fault, or I, for that matter.

SHANE

I'm not blaming anyone.

EUGENE

You two always blame others! But it's your own fault that you live meaningless lives. What do you expect me to do?

SHANE

I didn't mean to . . .

EUGENE

You never mean to . . . .

SHANE

. . . . the truth is, Dad, I couldn't take the sea. I only did it because I got so upset when they bombed Pearl Harbor, so I enlisted. That's when we tried that stuff as some kind of . . . pastime. But now I'm on my way back.

EUGENE

Back to what?

SHANE

Dad . . . I'm clean. You've got to believe me.

EUGENE

What's the use? It's stronger than you. It takes someone with a lot more guts than you'll ever have.

SHANE

I'm trying.

EUGENE

Yes, try, you try . . .

SHANE

I was nervous about coming here, because I knew you'd be angry no matter what I did.

EUGENE

Nobody asked you to come here.

SHANE

Dad, I've quit for good. You have to believe me. I'd rather cut my arm off.

EUGENE

Lies . . . lies I've heard nothing but lies since I was born. (*in a harsher tone of voice*) You don't want to . . . All you care about is that poison. You might as well be dead. (*looks at them*) I have no children. May God forgive me, but that's how I feel.

EUGENE JR.

Dad . . .

EUGENE

I didn't desert you, you deserted me. I can hardly walk. I don't know what's going on inside my brain. (*Eugene gets severe shakes.*) I've nothing to live for any more.

CARLOTTA

So die then, darling.

EUGENE JR.

Dad . . .

CARLOTTA

(*in a totally different tone of voice*) Did Cathy have any use for the layette I bought her?

EUGENE JR.

Dad . . .

EUGENE

I don't want to hear anything anymore.

CARLOTTA

Shane, I'm talking to you.

SHANE

Sorry?

(*Eugene walks over to the window, pulls the curtain. The room seems brighter and softer. A foghorn is heard. Carlotta puts her hand in front of her eyes.*)

CARLOTTA

Close the curtain! It's very unpleasant. (*Eugene lets go of the curtain.*) What's happening on Broadway these days?

EUGENE JR.

Broadway . . . Broadway theaters are filled with laughter—and outside misery reins.

CARLOTTA

I saw that "Death of a Salesman" has been a sell-out for six months. And Gene isn't there this year either.

EUGENE

I shouldn't ever have been there.

CARLOTTA

Nobody is asking for you, dear.

EUGENE JR.

(*quotes his father*) "He stood among them but not of them . . ."

CARLOTTA

They haven't asked for an O'Neill since "Days Without End," which was too long. Gene, your plays are too long.

EUGENE

Like my life. I don't need the theater. (*angrily*) I don't want to talk about it.

CARLOTTA

(*to Eugene Jr.*) Well, well, how quickly our heroes fade. Who remembers O'Neill? Just me. (*shakes off her thoughts*) I wouldn't mind going to the city sometime. I'd go directly to the Central Park Zoo. I've always loved monkeys . . . and dogs. I'm a monkey married to a dog. (*looks at Eugene*) No, I love him, I love him, I'm obsessed with that man!

EUGENE

(*to Eugene Jr.*) Did you see "Death of a Salesman"?

EUGENE JR.

No, I haven't yet.

EUGENE

Why not?

EUGENE JR.

Because I'm broke.

EUGENE

And you always will be. (*Eugene Jr. laughs.*) Don't think you'll get anything from me. There'll be nothing left when I'm gone.

CARLOTTA

We have nothing. We don't even have a car.

EUGENE JR.

I didn't come here to get anything . . .

CARLOTTA

Why not?

EUGENE JR.

You go to a father only when there's no one else to go to.

EUGENE

I'm almost penniless. And now, with these new taxes, I'll lose everything. I have to think about Carlotta and the time we have left.

EUGENE JR.

That's all right, Dad. Don't worry.

CARLOTTA

How nice of you to think of me.

EUGENE JR.

Next week I'm meeting with a guy who's producing radio commercials. I might make some money that way.

CARLOTTA

What are we going to live on? He doesn't want to sell his plays because he's insulted by the way they treat him.

EUGENE

They hate my plays, they destroy them. They don't want to hear the truth. They want laughs, tits and asses.

CARLOTTA

Still, he too has to eat, even though he's immortal! I'm trying to get him to write, not because of the money, but so that he'd be a little happier. (*to Eugene*) You are a hard man, Gene. And you're hiding plays, so that no one will know if they are good or bad. You'll soon be as forgotten as . . . Sam Behrman or Elmer Rice, or Odets!

EUGENE JR.

Odets was a socialist.

CARLOTTA

Who had cocktails at five in the Plaza bar. Those Bolsheviks, they fought the revolution at the Plaza hotel—Strasberg . . . Boleslavsky . . .

EUGENE

Odets was never close to a revolution his whole life. I knew poverty. "The Iceman Cometh" is really the only socialist play ever written in this country.

CARLOTTA

And that's the one that died on Broadway! They don't want to produce plays that don't return money.

EUGENE

These days there's more drama in the financing of a Broadway play than in the play itself.

CARLOTTA

Gene, we need money. I need money, you need money, not to mention Agnes and the others!

EUGENE

I'll never sell out. I saw what happened to my father. I promised myself that I'd never sell out. I don't belong on Broadway. I haven't set foot in a theater for ten years.

CARLOTTA

Just listen to him cutting off the goddamn branch he's sitting on. (*stamps her foot*) If you want to end up in some wretched poorhouse, do it, but don't drag me along!

EUGENE

They transform my words into graffiti on a urinal wall. We should have stayed in Provincetown.

CARLOTTA

Broadway is where there is real money.

EUGENE

Money. I've been at my desk since 1912. Every goddamn day for thirty years. What good did it do?

CARLOTTA

Now he starts with that again!

EUGENE

I see only failure and compromise. My plays—fifty, sixty thousand sheets of paper, sixty thousand corpses—for what?

CARLOTTA

You stopped writing just to torment me! I'll end my life in some horrible "old age home" without anyone to care for me.

EUGENE JR.

I thought you had a daughter?

CARLOTTA

I have no one! I have nothing!

EUGENE JR.

Cynthia. Isn't that her name?

CARLOTTA

(*furious*) I said, I have no one! Nothing! (*stomps her foot*) I've given everything I ever had to Eugene O'Neill! My church, my faith, my mother, my daughter and all my friends—sacrificed on his pagan altar! I've broken every one of the Ten Commandments for his sake! I can't even go to confession! I can't even get forgiveness—for his sins!

EUGENE

The mad scene, fifth act, "Electra."

CARLOTTA

I want to go home to New York. I wasn't made for a life in the country!

EUGENE JR.

Dad, that's a terrific idea, for you to move back to New York.

SHANE

Yes, then we could meet. Go to the movies.

EUGENE JR.

You'd feel better living there. Perhaps you'd start writing again. Dad, they haven't yet understood how great the "Iceman" is. A new generation will see what an extraordinary play it is . . . our only socialist play. It's like a novel . . . a Dostoyevsky novel.

EUGENE

With dialogue by Karl Marx. (*to Shane*) What's the matter with you?

SHANE

I'm fine.

EUGENE

A young man with your whole life ahead of you. What did you do upstairs? How do you take it?

SHANE

Nothing. I just went up and then I came down.

EUGENE

If you'd only stayed in the Navy . . . It's not my fault that you are the way you are. If I'd stayed with Agnes I would have died.

CARLOTTA

(*while caressing Estaban*) I'm not going to wander around this house all by myself like Mary in "Long Day's Journey" . . . without anything to hope for. (*suddenly in a different, rather unpleasant tone of voice to Eugene Jr.*) Do you make love to that woman, what's her name? (*short pause*) Did you screw her last night? (*Eugene Jr. doesn't know what to say and smiles.*) Isn't it wonderful . . . a really good lay? I miss it so. I'm as pure as Greta Garbo's pudenda. (*laughs*) But you probably don't have enough stamina for a real woman the way you drink.

EUGENE

Why the hell would it concern you?

CARLOTTA

He doesn't have the stamina. He hasn't done it for ten years, and before that it wasn't much to brag about either. Can you imagine—we haven't done it for ten years!

EUGENE JR.

(*wants to get up*) Well, for Christ's sake, let's go for a walk!

CARLOTTA

It was the same with Agnes.

EUGENE

Shut up, you old hag!

CARLOTTA

Poor Agnes . . . I hear she's writing a book about your marriage. What a thriller that'll be! (*laughs*) Why don't you go upstairs and write some goddamn masterpieces, so that we can get some money!

EUGENE JR.

Carlotta, you really are in a terrible mood.

CARLOTTA

My mood is of a woman who's been used and abused.

EUGENE

All you care about is money. (*Eugene tries to light a cigarette.*) We could sell *Long Day's Journey Into Night* if everything else fails.

EUGENE JR.

Is that a new play?

CARLOTTA

It's a damn old play. Good God, that'll be something for the gossip columnists to dig their teeth into.

EUGENE JR.

It sounds exciting. I'd like to read it.

EUGENE

If things get any worse we'll have to publish it.

CARLOTTA

Could it get any worse?

(*Shane lights a match and offers it to Eugene, who receives it with a shaky hand and lights his cigarette.*)

EUGENE JR.

Dad, may I read it?

EUGENE

(*Suddenly Eugene grabs Shane's hand. Shane tries to get out of his grip.*) Show me your arm.

EUGENE JR.

Dad!

SHANE

No.

(*Eugene let's go of his arm.*)

CARLOTTA

Why does it have to sit in a vault, when it could be out in the world making us money?

EUGENE

I don't want to see you anymore.

EUGENE JR.

Dad . . . take it easy.

EUGENE

And not you either!

SHANE

Dad, I haven't taken anything. It's true.

EUGENE

I don't give a damn!

SHANE

It's true.

(*He takes off his jacket, rolls up his shirtsleeves, shows his bare arms—everything in slow motion.*)

SHANE

Dad, look here. There's nothing. I haven't done anything.

EUGENE

I don't know how you did it, but I know you did it. You can't fool me.

EUGENE JR.

He's just nervous from being here.

SHANE

I haven't done anything, Dad. (*very upset*) Many times I've been close, but this time I've been strong—I fought it off. I haven't taken anything for six months. You must understand that I wouldn't do anything like that when I'm going to visit you. (*laughs a little*) All I did was sit on the train and come here, and we've been here the whole time. That's all.

CARLOTTA

(*picks up the telegrams from the table, then puts them down again*) Eugene O'Neill—wasn't he the Irishman who wrote a play in the twenties and they made it into a film with Greta Garbo . . . *Anna Christie*? Garbo they remember, but the playwright . . . Gene, you haven't had one production on Broadway in ten years—not counting "Iceman," which was the failure of the decade. You write a play about twelve bums babbling for six hours—no story, nothing! I begged you, Gene, don't do it, it'll fail—and I was right! When will you ever learn? People are tired of crying, they want to laugh.

EUGENE

I don't care.

CARLOTTA

I want to laugh! What do you care about?

EUGENE

Nothing.

(*Eugene stands up, is about to take a step forward but falls flat on the floor. Eugene Jr. hurries up to help him.*)

CARLOTTA

Look how the mighty fall. (*laughs*)

EUGENE JR.

Jesus, Carlotta . . . .

CARLOTTA

Where's your greatness now, little man?

EUGENE JR.

Stop it!

EUGENE

(*Eugene, his arms flailing, hits Eugene Jr., who is bending down to help him.*) Leave me alone, damn it!

EUGENE JR.

I just wanted to help you.

CARLOTTA

Leave him alone, everybody else does.

EUGENE

(*Eugene, into the carpet as he is trying to get up.*) Bitch! Whore! I can manage. I don't need any help. (*He stands up slowly, collects himself.*)

CARLOTTA

Day's without end at the O'Neill's. (*laughs*)

EUGENE

(*to Eugene Jr.*) It's all right. I just fell. My body, it doesn't obey any longer. (*He stands up, about to go upstairs.*)

CARLOTTA

Where do you think you're going?

EUGENE

I'm not talking to you, you old whore. (*He walks towards the stairs.*)

CARLOTTA

Well, good. That's good. (*in a different tone of voice*) Don't be silly, Gene. A whore is a woman who sleeps with men. (*She stands up and follows Eugene half way up the stairs.*) I'm going to talk to my lawyer about suing you and Saxe Commins. That'll be a court case that'll make Hiroshima look like a Disney movie! (*She runs upstairs.*)

EUGENE

Do whatever the hell you want!

(*There are sounds of a fistfight.*)

EUGENE JR.

Holy mother, my God, my God . . . . Are they really going at each other?

CARLOTTA

Don't you dare hit me! (*screams*) You're hurting me!

EUGENE

That's the idea! (*silence*)

EUGENE JR.

Oh my God . . . my God! (*laughs, shakes his head*) It's worse than I thought.

SHANE

How long are we staying?

EUGENE JR.

I thought we were the bad guys . . . . (*He walks over to the table with the whiskey bottles.*)

SHANE

Do we have to stay the whole goddamn day? I want to go back to the city.

EUGENE JR.

I need another drink. Leave whenever the hell you like. She asks me if I'm screwing Ruth! Jesus Christ! (*He serves himself a drink.*)

EUGENE JR.

She's killing him. (*He walks back, drinks, puts the glass down, takes a cigarette out of Eugene's cigarette holder, and puts five cigarettes in his pocket.*) He doesn't have a lot of time left. I wonder if we'll inherit anything . . . other than a bad reputation. But what good would it do me? You could use some money. (*He looks around the room.*) God, what a place. A mausoleum. Mourning becomes Electra.

SHANE

Yes.

EUGENE JR.

"Mourning Becomes Electra." (*short pause*) The best one he ever wrote. (*looks at Shane*) What the hell are we doing here? (*laughs*) I always have this hope that I can talk to him, that I can try to make him understand.

SHANE

Understand what?

EUGENE JR.

I don't know. (*short pause*) When I went to the Trinity School I did real well. They predicted I would have a brilliant future. (*sees Shane is shaking lightly*) You have to do something about those shakes.

SHANE

I have a problem with my blood circulation.

EUGENE JR.

Do you want to go for a walk? It'll be good for you. *Currite, noctis equi*
... the fresh air. It's the only thing we'll enjoy around here.

SHANE

Couldn't we leave soon? I can't manage much longer.

EUGENE JR.

What do you mean?

SHANE

It's worse than I thought. I've got to have one ...

EUGENE JR.

Here? In Dad's house? With him upstairs? You're crazy.

SHANE

I won't make it.

EUGENE JR.

Jesus Christ, Shane ... think about it.

SHANE

It's physical. It's not mental. It's the body, not me.

EUGENE JR.

Do what you have to do ... but not here ... not now.

SHANE

I'm not really hooked. It's only because I'm here.

EUGENE JR.

It's your life.

SHANE

Yes, sadly ... this is really my life.

EUGENE JR.

If I were you, I'd switch tracks.

SHANE

I would too ...

EUGENE JR.

I'm going to switch tracks soon. Before I turn forty. In some dashing manner. The classical way . . . Roman fashion . . . bathtub . . . wrists . . .

SHANE

What's that?

EUGENE JR.

I guess it's a joke. (*He looks on as Shane bends down, takes off his left shoe, gets out a small bag with drug paraphernalia, then turns up the leg of his pants, pulls off his tie and knots it around his upper thigh.*) Is that stuff expensive?

SHANE

Five bucks.

EUGENE JR.

Five bucks?

SHANE

It used to be two bucks.

SHANE

(*Shane points the needle straight to his heart and says jokingly*) If I do it here, it's "Good bye, Charlie." (*He injects the needle in his left leg, waits for the desired result, puts the stuff back in the bag, puts the shoe back on, and sinks back into the sofa.*)

EUGENE JR.

What happens now?

SHANE

If the stuff is good, I feel good. (*smiles*) Sometimes I hope I'll overdose without meaning to.

EUGENE JR.

Wouldn't that be nice. What about Cathy, and the kids, and Dad?

SHANE

Dad doesn't give a shit about me. He wouldn't care if I didn't exist.

EUGENE JR.

How can you say that? You're his favorite.

SHANE

I've hardly spent any time with him. I visited him in different places. I told him I changed schools . . . I joined the Navy . . . that we were on our way to Iwo Jima, and now I'm married, and now I have a child, Eugene the third . . . and now we have one more child. (*laughs*) He always thought I was nice, but worthless. I guess he was right.

EUGENE JR.

Put your shoe back on.

SHANE

I will. (*laughs quietly*) I, too, read quite a lot. I liked reading. Now I like movies. I hardly ever go to the theater. (*quietly*) I'll tell you one thing—I never liked his plays. The last one I saw was the Greek one, the one you were talking about, but I thought it was . . . dull. Good story. But I didn't feel anything. I did like "Ah, Wilderness!" That was a good one. In that one I recognized things. It's strange that he wrote that one.

EUGENE JR.

It's a comedy.

SHANE

He doesn't write for the people in this country, for people like me or the ones I know. (*pause*) When I was at Lexington for detox, most of the people there wanted to get away from it . . . but I didn't. What would I do then? (*laughs*) When I was in the Navy I read Nietzsche. I thought it was the right read before going ashore to kill. He talked about the love of one's fate, to follow the star of one's destiny, wherever it takes you.

EUGENE JR.

Amor fati, love of one's fate.

SHANE

Maybe there are some with such a star. I don't have one. Unless Dad is my star. He was never a Dad.

EUGENE JR.

Do you think I've had a Dad? The first twelve years of my life I thought my last name was Fitzgimmon. Eugene Fitzgimmon, the world's nicest guy, an ordinary goddamn Jersey kid.

SHANE

Cheap marijuana cigarettes in the Navy, there was nothing else to do. I smoked because everybody else did. It was pretty nice to spend the whole day in the hammock, getting a suntan and watching your dreams drift away with the smoke. (*smiles softly*) I, too, am a poet. I even thought of becoming an actor once upon a time.

EUGENE JR.

Sure.

SHANE

An actor or an author. To write about people living in nature. I wrote to Dad asking for some help. He wrote back that I was much too lazy to do anything like that. I've never been lazy. (*feeling sleepy and numb*) I was just drifting around for a while, then I applied to a Military Academy . . . and then came Pearl Harbor . . . Thank God.

EUGENE JR.

I had a dad who wasn't my dad, and then I got another one who was my dad, and then all of a sudden they were both gone.

SHANE

To me life was always like a book, which I'll start reading one of these days.

EUGENE JR.

I didn't mind Fitzgimmon. He was a regular blue-collar guy . . . the only remarkable thing in his life was that he was sleeping with a woman who had slept with Eugene O'Neill. (*short pause*) One day my mom brought me to a fancy hotel on Broadway and told me that I was going to meet someone who was my father. Take the elevator, she said, I'll be waiting for you. I went up and knocked on the door and he opened it. He looked at me and told me to come in. I don't know if I even dared to look at him. He told me who he was, that he was a writer and that he'd been sick so that he hadn't been able to be there for me, that he'd been in the jungle looking for gold, but now he was writing plays. He asked me what school I was going to and if I had a lot of friends. Then he said it had been fun to see me and gave me five dollars. (*He walks over to the fireplace, looks at the photographs on the mantel, and picks one up.*) This one is from France, from the castle, where we visited him when he had married her. . . . That was the first time I met you. (*short pause*) Do you remember?

SHANE

Yes . . . we went swimming.

EUGENE JR.

He worked the whole time. The only time we saw Dad and Carlotta was at meal time, and then we were afraid to speak. It was awful.

(*Shane puts his jacket on backwards without noticing and tries to find the buttons. Eugene Jr. goes behind him and ties the jacket sleeves together and starts to laugh.*)

SHANE

Cut it out.

EUGENE JR.

You're going straight to Bellevue.

SHANE

Fine with me. I like those places. Peaceful and calm.

EUGENE JR.

How the hell is it possible to put a jacket on backwards? There must be something wrong with you, Shane.

SHANE

I'm too good for this world. Cathy says I'm like a character in a Dostoyevsky novel.

EUGENE JR.

"The Idiot."

SHANE

That's right. That one I've read. (*starts to laugh more and more*)

EUGENE JR.

What's so funny? Stop it Shane!

SHANE

(*wipes away tears*) Yes, I know . . . when I start I can't stop.

(*Eugene enters carrying a thin manuscript and looks at them with an almost remorseful expression. Shane stops laughing.*)

EUGENE

It was long ago that I heard someone laugh in this house. (*tries to smile*) What's going on, what's so funny?

EUGENE JR.

Shane told a funny story. Did you get a little rest?

EUGENE

No, I took a look at this one. (*about the manuscript*) Shane . . .

SHANE

Yes, Dad. (*looks at Eugene, smiles*) Here I am.

EUGENE

Shane . . . I'm sorry I said what I said. I didn't mean to. It doesn't help. (*Shane shakes his head.*) It has to do with what I experienced as a child. I don't want to get into it. You can't possibly have sunk so low that it's too late . . . if you really want to get away from it . . . and I hope to God you will.

SHANE

That's all right, Dad. It's all right.

EUGENE

I haven't been the kind of father you needed. . . . Artists shouldn't have children. But I've tried. That's all I can say.

SHANE

Yes, Dad. I know.

EUGENE JR.

Sure you did.

EUGENE

I have tried.

SHANE

I know.

EUGENE

I've never known what it is to grow up in a proper home. (*He gives Eugene Jr. the manuscript.*) I've written a play about it. I call it "Long Day's Journey into Night." I want you to take a look at it. To read it. Would you like to?

EUGENE JR.

Me? Of course I would, Dad! Thank you.

EUGENE

You can't take it home with you. This is the original.

EUGENE JR.

Terrific! Wonderful! Would you like me to read it now? Of course! I'll start right away. (*He flips through the manuscript.*) Your writing gets smaller and smaller. (*He reads, lifting the pages up towards the light.*) What does it say here?

EUGENE

Fool . . . you're a sentimental fool. (*from memory*) "What is so wonderful about that first meeting between a silly romantic schoolgirl and a matinee idol? You were much happier before you knew he existed, in the convent when you used to pray to the Blessed Virgin." That's mother. The third act. In here is everything I've tried to say but never managed for forty years. (*bitterly*) I thought that the truth was the only thing worth searching for. It was when the war broke out and the whole world went mad that I gave up all hope that the theater could change anything. The world became mute and I became deaf—what I wrote and thought didn't matter any longer. That's when I could finally tell my story—no more masks, disguises or devices. I could finally see them as they were. (*in a different tone of voice*) Perhaps in thirty years it could be published as a book. That might be better than having it performed by careless actors. . . . (*to Eugene Jr.*) I don't want you to talk about the play, not a word to anyone, do you understand?

EUGENE JR.

Yes, of course, I won't talk to anyone about it. (*happily*) Thank you, Dad. It's like a gift.

EUGENE

Don't say anything to Carlotta, either. She's silly that way. (*looks into the darkened hallway*) One would think that the only time she was happy was at the convent and in her childhood home.

EUGENE JR.

May I read it upstairs in your study? May I take a drink with me upstairs? (*laughs*) I have a feeling I'll need it.

EUGENE

(*to Shane*) I'll let you read it some other time, but I thought Gene should read it first.

SHANE

That's fine.

EUGENE JR.

I'm going upstairs.

EUGENE

(*Eugene walks over to one of the windows and opens the curtain.*) Always the same damn fog. (*pause*) She could be so evil and cold, and then the very next moment an innocent, beguiling girl, who didn't understand anything. (*laughs*) She was the real actress—much more skilled than Papa! (*Suddenly he notices Shane.*)

Shane . . . (*He walks over to him.*) Shane.

SHANE

That's all right. . . . It's hard for me to read. Where's everybody?

EUGENE

Carlotta is resting. (*short pause*) So that she'll have the strength to be even meaner later on. (*laughs*)

SHANE

Aha! . . . Could I have a cigarette? (*Shane takes a cigarette, lights it, and smiles at Eugene.*)

EUGENE

Well, it's been a while.

SHANE

Sure has.

EUGENE

Yes. (*short pause*) She sleeps with a poker next to her bed.

SHANE

Who? Why?

EUGENE

And I have a Remington. But I have no ammunition. Well, that's how it is. (*pause*) When mother had taken that poison, we used to pretend that we hadn't noticed; then she would go back upstairs again. (*pause*) I don't even know where you live.

SHANE

Where I've always lived.

EUGENE

I've never been there.

SHANE

No. But I still live there.

EUGENE

Aha.

SHANE

Yea. We have no plans to move.

EUGENE

How is . . . what's her name . . .

SHANE

Who? Cathy?

EUGENE

I didn't forget her name. But I can't remember it. . . . Cathy, that's right.
How is she?

SHANE

She's fine.

EUGENE

I remember her very well. (*pause*) A nice girl. (*pause*) It's good that you
stay together. A nice girl. . . . Is she working?

SHANE

Cathy? Yes, she is.

EUGENE

So, you do manage?

SHANE

Yeh, sure.

EUGENE

That's good.

SHANE

I'll find something . . . to do too, when I feel a little stronger.

EUGENE

She seemed so nice. . . . (*pause*) She looked like Agnes.

SHANE

Mom? Cathy? Mom?

EUGENE

She's the very image of Agnes, when we first met in the Village. Agnes
was like a cool breeze. I was a restless, dour son of a bitch, consumed by
work. I hope she's doing all right. I've heard she's writing a book.
(*pause*) And you're married to a girl who reads poetry and who likes
Yeats and Edna St. Vincent.

SHANE

There's not a lot of poetry these days.

EUGENE

How do you manage in New York? If you wanted to, you could've stayed out at sea.

SHANE

I do all kinds of things. I'm trying to get it together . . . I go to the movies.

EUGENE

The ocean is the best place for people who are afraid and unhappy. I went out to sea and tried to manage by myself. I learned what it meant to work like a dog . . . . But I never believed that booze and narcotics would be the solution. (*pause*) I'm not scolding you, Shane.

SHANE

I had enough of the sea in the Navy.

EUGENE

I spent the First World War in a sanatorium. Coughed too damn much to go out fighting. I was so proud when you wrote that you had enlisted in the Navy. I thought about you during the whole war, and I was right there with you . . . even if that might sound pathetic.

SHANE

Yes, of course you were!

EUGENE

I told you it was pathetic. It must've been hell.

SHANE

One gets used to it.

EUGENE

You did something, anyway.

SHANE

I didn't do anything special.

EUGENE

And now what?

SHANE

What? (*pause*) Dad . . . what's there to say?

EUGENE

Tell me the truth, damn it.

SHANE

What truth?

EUGENE

Are you really trying to stop using . . . that . . .?

SHANE

Of course I am. Sure I am.

EUGENE

There must be someone who could help you.

SHANE

Yes, sure there is.

EUGENE

Cathy . . . Agnes . . . God.

SHANE

So there really is a God?

EUGENE

When I think about how Mama fought against that tyranny for twenty-five years . . . and then I get a son who becomes an addict! Are you that weak, Shane? I hate to think you are.

SHANE

I've quit, Dad. I can quit. It just takes a little time.

EUGENE

Don't fool yourself!

SHANE

No. (*laughs*) I hope you're wrong. Grandma managed.

EUGENE

You are not her! She didn't know how dangerous it was, until it was too late. Morphine was as easy to get as quinine. She didn't get away from it until Papa died. (*pause*) It's just that I'd hoped it would end with me. Don't you understand what you're doing?

SHANE

Yeh. . . . (*pause*) Did you ever see Eugene?

EUGENE

What? Who?

SHANE

The baby who died. We named him Eugene the third. After you. did you ever see him?

EUGENE

No.

SHANE

We had just gotten an apartment in New York. On Bleecker Street. (*pause*) Are you writing anything now? (*pause*) Are you writing a new play? (*pause*) I'll go and look for Gene. I want to ask him when we're leaving.

(*Shane leaves. Eugene gets up and follows Shane up the stairs. The stage is empty for a short while. Then Saki comes in and starts to straighten out the room. He is about to take some glasses and ashtrays to the kitchen when he hears someone coming down the stairs. He sees Eugene and bows. Eugene is carrying a big pack of manuscripts.*)

SAKI

Is there anything I can do for you, sir?

EUGENE

(*Eugene walks over to the fireplace and puts one of the manuscripts in the fire without looking at it.*) No thank you, nothing.

(*He puts one manuscript after another in the fire. Carlotta comes downstairs. She has changed her clothes, is wearing a sheer black blouse, black skirt, and has put on makeup and styled her hair in such a way that she looks very much like the actress Alla Nazimova, who played Christine in "Mourning Becomes Electra." She stops, looks at Eugene and recites from the play.*)

CARLOTTA

"I'll live alone with the dead. I'll never go out or see anyone! I'll have shutters nailed closed so no sunlight can ever get in. I'll live alone with the dead, and keep their secrets, and let them hound me, until the curse is paid out and the last Mannon is let die." (*She waits in the middle of the room.*) Don't you think I look beautiful? Don't you see who I look like? I dressed up—like death. I thought it would cheer you up a little. (*laughs*) Everybody said she was prepared to give her life for the role in "Electra." It wasn't worth it. I should have done it.

EUGENE

I'm burning my plays . . . every one.

CARLOTTA

(*Carlotta walks closer to him.*) Yes, I know. It smells like burning corpses.

EUGENE

The whole cycle.

CARLOTTA

Yes, why not? If a few million Jews could burn, why not a few worthless plays? (*She walks over to him.*) May I help you? (*She takes one of the manuscripts from him.*) And give us the shadows . . . and give us death.

SCENE TWO

(*Carlotta is the only one left in the unlit room. She is sitting in the chair looking on as the final papers go up in smoke.*)

CARLOTTA

(*quietly*) I wish I could disappear like that . . . (*pause*) Saki! Saki! Please come! (*Saki enters.*) Give me a little whiskey. It'll warm me up, if nothing else. Make it a full glass, please. What would I do without you?

God knows. (*She receives the glass.*) I have nothing against stimulants—
that stimulate. Please, Saki, sit down, you don't have to keep standing
when we're alone. (*Saki slowly sits down. Impulsively she reaches out
for his hand.*) Now he's burning his plays. He's burning ten whole years.
. . . (*laughs*) If I were a play he would've burnt me too. (*She takes Saki's
hand and caresses it.*) I'll end up in some home for the aged. No one will
take care of me. I had a daughter, but she hates me. That's Gene's fault.
She could have stayed with me and taken care of me when I get old—but
Gene pushed her away. Come and sit a little closer. (*Suddenly she pushes
her bosom out, turns slightly, and shakes her body somewhat.*) How do
you like them? You can touch them if you want to. Please go ahead. I'm
still attractive, don't you think? (*She takes his hand and laughs*) I'm like
a desert. When will I bloom? And still, I've never been unfaithful.

SAKI

Sorry, ma'am. (*stands up*) I have to go and help Doris take out the
garbage.

CARLOTTA

The garbage?

SAKI

Yes, ma'am.

CARLOTTA

I have a lot more interesting garbage than Doris.

SAKI

Sorry, ma'am.

CARLOTTA

Do you have something going with Doris?

SAKI

Ma'am?

CARLOTTA

Of course you do! I can understand it gets lonely out here for a good-
looking young man like you. The garbage—that's the silliest thing I've
ever heard in my whole life!

SAKI

Yes, ma'am.

CARLOTTA

My God . . . I can still drive any man crazy. Well, leave then, if you think it's more fun with that fat little bitch! Leave! (*Saki bows and leaves. Carlotta hears footsteps in the dark.*) Gene? (*pause*) What do you want? (*pause*) What is it, Gene? (*pause*) Leave me alone. (*pause*) I can't take it anymore. Go away!

EUGENE JR.

(*with a thick voice*) It's me.

CARLOTTA

Who?

EUGENE JR.

It's me, Carlotta. Eugene, the young one.

CARLOTTA

Go away. I don't want to see anyone!

EUGENE JR.

Me neither. (*He turns on the ceiling light.*)

CARLOTTA

No, turn that off! I can't stand the light.

EUGENE JR.

(*Eugene Jr. turns the light off.*) I was just going to wet my whistle.

CARLOTTA

You're already drunk.

EUGENE JR.

I'm not drunk, unfortunately. I never get drunk. Where's everybody?

CARLOTTA

I don't know why you drag him up here, when you know how he is.

EUGENE JR.

(*Eugene Jr. makes himself a drink and drinks.*) Carlotta, I'm not going to discuss anything with you. (*pause*) Do you know where I've been? I've been to Knossos. I've been there an hour longer than life itself. I've walked up from the beach to the castle where the monarchs live . . . where the gods don't interfere, because they see that the games the mortals play are divine and terrifying. They take pleasure, as if it were the evening breeze, in the meaningless screams of mortals. I have been with Aeschylus. I have been with my father for the first and only time. I've been crying like a child. (*pours himself another drink.*) Now I'm going to drink as much as I possibly can—if nothing else. I'll have more tears that way. Never again do I want to come home.

CARLOTTA

Have you gone mad?

EUGENE JR.

I will never come home.

CARLOTTA

And this is supposed to be his birthday—perhaps his last. He has decided that he's going to die now. He has burned his plays—the whole big cycle he had worked on for fifteen years. Thousands of pages. Now I'm the only one left.

EUGENE JR.

You'll manage all right.

SHANE

(*Shane enters, he is in a good mood.*) There you are! I've been looking for you everywhere. Aren't we leaving soon? Gene?

CARLOTTA

Yes, why don't you.

SHANE

Aren't we going home soon?

EUGENE JR.

Home? I have no home.

CARLOTTA

He'll never forgive you.

EUGENE JR.

No. (*laughs*) He'll never forgive us, for abandoning us.

EUGENE

(*Eugene enters.*)Why the hell is it so dark everywhere? (*He walks around the room turning on all the lights.*) What are you up to?

EUGENE JR.

Planning the murder of Caesar.

EUGENE

Are you capable of that? (*short pause*) Are you already drunk?

EUGENE JR.

No, no, but I had to have a drink after finishing reading the play.

CARLOTTA

Which play?

EUGENE JR.

I don't know what to say. . . . . It's incredible, fantastic, unbelievable. It's a real killer-diller, Dad.

CARLOTTA

Is it "Long Day's Journey into Night?"

EUGENE

What kind of language is that? Killer-diller?

EUGENE JR.

It's the greatest play ever written. It's incredible, Dad.

EUGENE

I know.

CARLOTTA

You gave it to HIM?

EUGENE JR.

I've only read the first and the last act. The rest I can fill in myself.

CARLOTTA

You promised me you'd never show it to a living soul!

EUGENE JR.
I'm not ashamed to admit it, but I sat upstairs and cried.

EUGENE
Let's not talk about it now. (*He sits down in his chair but doesn't look at Carlotta, who is getting very upset.*) I don't want to talk about it. (*looks up*) Was someone upstairs earlier?

EUGENE JR.
But Dad . . . do you think you'll get it published, the way it reads right now? Isn't it too powerful?

EUGENE
Someone was upstairs. There was someone walking around up there.

SHANE
I was there, Dad. A little while ago. I was looking for you all.

CARLOTTA
How could you? That's our play, our child.

EUGENE
It's my play. Everything I've ever written is mine, mine alone!

CARLOTTA
I've carried it like a child. I helped you give birth to it—and you gave it to me as a gift. It's the only love I've ever received from you. In the dedication it says, it's a tribute to my love and affection. On our wedding anniversary in 1942.

EUGENE
At that time we still had hope.

CARLOTTA
You said that I gave you the courage to confront your dead ones and finally dare to write about them. "These twelve years, my beloved, that we have lived together, have been a journey into light—into love." (*starts to cry*)

EUGENE
Now there isn't much light left.

CARLOTTA

There's nothing left.

EUGENE JR.

Dad, please listen. It's something I've been longing to tell you. I'm an ant crawling at your feet. I'm nothing compared to you. You know how proud I am of you. I always have been. This is a masterpiece. It's about me. It's about my life, Dad, my thoughts, my feelings . . . as strange as it may sound. (*pause*) I've experienced everything you wrote about. I am Jamie. I've always known that I'm Jamie. Only a god could write like this. I'm so proud to have your blood in my veins. It's been like a dark divine presence. But Dad, I beg you, dear Dad . . . you have to hold off publishing this play.

CARLOTTA

We'll publish it whenever we want to!

EUGENE JR.

You see . . . if this comes out, my chances at the network will be in jeopardy. This is strong stuff.

CARLOTTA

Your chances at the network?

EUGENE

You have no chances . . . anywhere.

EUGENE JR.

No, I'm a real ass. What right do I have to be alive? (*He drinks.*) I'm an idiot coming here thinking I could establish some kind of contact.

CARLOTTA

You have exactly what you deserve, both of you.

EUGENE

Stop it now, goddamnit.

CARLOTTA

One is an alcoholic and the other is a drug addict, and the old man is whining about his mama.

EUGENE

You wretched old bitch, I'll kill you.

CARLOTTA

Everybody thinks that what he needs is a nice little wife adoring him. Bullshit! He needs hell—so that he can write about it.

EUGENE

Shut up!

CARLOTTA

He needs me to punish him in order to survive. But God in heaven, what a high price I've had to pay! I could've become a great actress.

EUGENE

You? A great actress? (*to Eugene Jr.*) They called her the Hottentott actress. Because her legs were short and crooked.

CARLOTTA

Shut up. The papers said that I was one of the most beautiful actresses on Broadway! People couldn't understand why I fell for a son of a bitch like you! I must've been drugged!

EUGENE

The kind of actress who was given the role of "gold digger," the best friend with very few lines. When she opened her mouth her voice was loud and stilted.

CARLOTTA

Shut up, you damn idiot!

EUGENE

Believe me, you had no talent, you would never have made it.

CARLOTTA

And you aren't a playwright, either! Just an hysterical old maid, stone cold dead, without a soul!

EUGENE

I am free. Nothing else matters. The theater robs your life. It ransacks your most profound insights and uses them as popular clichés. You work for years on something that has the strength and spirituality of a miracle that they transform into a cheap theatrical trick. Nothing is sacred. . . . Of all my plays there was only one production and only one actor who fully realized what I had intended . . . Charles Gilpin in "Emperor Jones."

CARLOTTA

That insane Negro. What the hell does that tell you? A Negro being the best thing in your play? The real actors refused. Someone wrote that it was impossible to judge your plays: "Who can judge a symphony by a tone deaf composer." (*laughs*) That's wonderful!

EUGENE JR.

Why then has he received such adulation?

SHANE

He did get the Nobel Prize.

CARLOTTA

I was beautiful, independent, with my whole life ahead of me! Why did I get involved with you! I'm not a masochist! I thought I could help you!

EUGENE

She said the money came from an aunt in California, but that was a lie, that too.

CARLOTTA

I never said that!

EUGENE

It didn't come from any aunt in California—it came from one of her old lovers, Speyer, who paid for her services.

CARLOTTA

What are you saying?

EUGENE

From that dirty old fart, Speyer, with whom I was sharing her . . .

CARLOTTA

Don't you dare, you son of a bitch!

EUGENE

She was a whore already.

CARLOTTA

Let him be! Let him rest in peace!

EUGENE

Two customers, me and Speyer. . . . Ralph Barton was a homo.
Everybody knew that, except her.

CARLOTTA

He wasn't any more of a homo than you are! You're a homo!

EUGENE JR.

Please calm down, both of you.

CARLOTTA

Well boys, do you know why we separated for a while, your dad and I?
I'll tell you. I just happened to come home when he obviously didn't
expect me. Do you know what he was doing . . . in our bed, in that hotel
in New York! Well, I found your father in bed with one of our best
friends—an editor! And they were naked! I just turned around and left.

EUGENE

That's a lie.

CARLOTTA

I'll never forget what I saw.

EUGENE

Lies . . . lies . . . lies . . .

SHANE

Can't you stop it now!

CARLOTTA

I could vomit.

EUGENE

You're rotten to the core, filthy old slut!

CARLOTTA

You ought to be ashamed of yourself, Eugene O'Neill! Speyer was a real man, a real gentleman, educated and elegant and well spoken. . . . He never asked for those filthy things you forced me to do to you, that made me forget God!

EUGENE

Hallucinations . . . Lady Macbeth.

CARLOTTA

You're the one hallucinating! Do you really think I'll continue to wash your shitty underwear, powder your ass and play canasta for the rest of my life? (*She runs over to the fireplace, takes the photograph of Eugene and his mother, throws it on the floor and steps on the broken glass.*)

EUGENE

That's all you're good for.

CARLOTTA

That's it! Your damn kids can take care of you! I want my money back! I sold everything I had in order to buy this house, and I haven't gotten a cent for more than twenty years work! You even stole my words! And you talk about actors being vampires! I hate you! I'm taking you to court.

EUGENE JR.

(*Eugene Jr. blows slowly three times into an empty whiskey bottle.*) "Long day's journey into night"—Dad, did you hear? (*blows three more times.*) Yeh, yeh . . .

EUGENE

You're more believable when you say you hate me than when you say you love me.

CARLOTTA

(*quietly, calmly*) I can't any more. I've given you twenty years of my life to make you happy, but it was all wasted. (*She pulls off her wedding band.*) You've hurt me more than I can say.

EUGENE

(*Eugene looks at her as she puts the ring on the table.*) Carlotta. Forgive me. I didn't mean it. Forgive me for all the pain I've caused you.

CARLOTTA

Not even God would.

EUGENE

I have nothing left. I've burnt my plays. I won't live much longer.

CARLOTTA

Thank God.

EUGENE

Carlotta.

CARLOTTA

I don't want to live here anyway. I want to live where there's people.

EUGENE

I'll do whatever you want. Just don't leave me.

CARLOTTA

What about the plays? Who'll get them?

EUGENE

It doesn't matter . . . I'll never write again. No one really cares about them.

CARLOTTA

I'll take care of them then.

EUGENE

Everything is a lie. The plays are tombs of lives I've never lived. Lies, lies. I'll never forgive you. Jamie can take you home. He can bury you, if you were to ever die. You never did take care of me when I was little . . . you never did. I had to fend for myself. I walked around with a fever of a hundred and four, coughing up blood, but you weren't there. I couldn't free myself of you. I couldn't free myself without getting crushed . . . can't purify my blood from yours, can't untangle your thoughts and feelings from mine. The only time that exists is that which we shared under the same roof—the same long day from morning to night. Thousands of days, all the same day. You tell me that all your misfortunes are my fault, you say that if I hadn't been born you wouldn't have had to suffer as you do now. . . . Father always takes your side. He says it's Jamie's fault; that even though he had the measles, went into Edmund's room and infected him, so that he died, because Jamie wanted you all to himself. Jamie taught me everything. He found me my first whore . . . the only thing I had to find out for myself was how you were. You were supposed to be my mother, my home, my house. . . . You got satisfaction from tormenting us. The look in your eyes when you leave us . . . when you don't give a damn about us! I loved you, I loved your smile. Those first summers in New London, when we were all together, when I sat on the rocks, gazing out over the ocean and listening to you playing the piano back in the house. I never felt such happiness.

CARLOTTA

(*Carlotta walks over to Eugene and hugs him.*) There, Gene, there, there. Everything will be all right. (*She holds his shaking hands.*) Now everything is fine. Gene, don't think about all that now. It's old and forgotten.

EUGENE

No.

CARLOTTA

Old and forgotten.

EUGENE

No.

CARLOTTA

There, there.

EUGENE

Yes. Carlotta, don't leave.

CARLOTTA

Where the hell would I go?

EUGENE

Stay with me . . .

CARLOTTA

Yes, yes.

EUGENE

You are my mother now.

CARLOTTA

I'm your mother now.

EUGENE

The only one I have.

CARLOTTA

No, stop it! (*She pushes him away when he tries to hold her.*) I'm not your mother!

EUGENE

I've burned everything. There's nothing left. I only want to be with you. You're the only one I've ever loved. I can't live without you, Carlotta.

CARLOTTA

I don't want to be your mother, if you're this naughty.

EUGENE JR.

(*Eugene Jr. looks at his watch.*) I hate to leave a party, especially one as stimulating as this, but it's getting late. Well, Dad, as we were saying . . . we're on our way.

EUGENE

Yes.

EUGENE JR.

Yes, Dad.

SHANE

Yes. Cathy might get worried.

CARLOTTA

Saki! Saki!

EUGENE JR.

It was nice to see you, anyway.

(*Saki enters.*)

SHANE

Yes.

CARLOTTA

Saki, please call for a cab.

EUGENE JR.

Maybe we'll see you both in New York sometime. It would be fun.

EUGENE

(*Eugene takes out a checkbook from his inner pocket.*) Wait. (*short pause*) Maybe you need . . . a little something. I'll write you a check . . . some money.

EUGENE JR.

No, Dad, you don't have to.

SHANE

Thank you, very kind of you.

EUGENE

For our grandchildren . . .

CARLOTTA

Eugene Jr. doesn't have any children, as far as we know.

EUGENE

Now that he's getting married, anything is possible.

SHANE

I have children.

CARLOTTA

How much did you give away?

EUGENE

Five hundred. Is that enough?

EUGENE JR.

Sure, Dad. That'll go a long way.

EUGENE

(*Eugene gives Eugene Jr. the check.*) Buy the kids something, or take them to a fun movie.

EUGENE JR.

Thank you.

CARLOTTA

From Grandpa.

SHANE

It's too much.

EUGENE JR.

It's been very nice. I hope you feel better soon.

SAKI

(*Saki enters.*) The cab is here.

EUGENE

Give Oona my regards when you see her.

SHANE

I will . . . I hope I'll see her soon.

EUGENE JR.

Goodbye, Dad. It was wonderful to see you. And the play is fantastic. Good bye, Dad.

EUGENE

Goodbye.

SHANE

Thank you.

(*They leave.*)

CARLOTTA

Well, well. (*pause*) That's that. (*pause*) Gene, what do you think of us getting a new dog? A little puppy to play with? (*pause*) No . . . you don't want to. You don't want to do anything. You don't want to talk . . . you don't want to live. . . . You used to smile sometimes, once a year maybe.

A smile that made you look so young and beautiful. (*pause*) Gene, dear, promise me you won't get up tonight. I need to sleep, Gene. (*pause*) But Gene, do say something. (*pause*) Everything would be much simpler if I didn't love you so. (*pause*) The most wonderful gift you've ever given me is "Long Day's Journey into Night." (*pause*) I cried when I read it. (*pause*) I cried the whole morning.

THE END

Autumn and Winter

Characters

Margareta: The Mother, in her mid 60s

Henrick: The Father, in his early 70s

Eva: A Daughter, in her early 40s

Ann: A Daughter, in her mid 30s

The setting is a family dinner at the parents' apartment.

MARGARETA

You don't like it?

EVA

I don't think I want . . .

ANN

I do, but I got some— what do you call it?— ointment . . . in my mouth.

EVA

I don't think so.

MARGARETA

I really tried to make something you'd like. I made an effort.

HENRICK

Maybe you aren't hungry.

ANN

One has to be.

EVA

Effort.

ANN

Sacrifice.

EVA

Endeavor.

ANN

Tastes like an endeavor too. Peter bought something to put on John's nails, since he's also added that to his repertoire. I used some of that stuff and now I got it in my mouth.

EVA

(*about the salad*) I don't know. Maybe.

HENRICK

Do you still bite your nails?

MARGARETA

Not Ann, John!

EVA

No, that's hard to stop.

ANN

Yes. . . . The other day I tested a salad dressing, and it tasted so strange that I said to Robert, the chef, "What terrible dressing you made." But then I realized I had tasted that ointment. (*pours herself some wine*) But who said it was supposed to be easy? Right, Dad?

MARGARETA

(*in a friendly voice*) You've really got to stop that, biting your nails, I mean. Let me look at them.

ANN

(*to Henrick*) More wine? . . . No, you may not.

MARGARETA

They'll get so strange looking.

EVA

Weren't we told that all the time . . . that it was supposed to be so easy?

MARGARETA

It's a very bad habit.

EVA

But I can't do anything about it now.

HENRICK

(*puts his hand over his glass*) No thank you, I'm fine.

MARGARETA

Could there be anything genetic or inherited in biting your nails? Henrick often does it too, when he's thinking of something . . . in the evenings.

ANN

Mother? (*about the wine*)

EVA

Do you, Dad?

MARGARETA

Thank you, dear. Henrick is supposed to drink and look a little happy.
Henrick, my dear, be a little happy.

HENRICK

I am happy, Margareta.

MARGARETA

Since our girls are here.

ANN

He's together with this girl that everybody thinks is so sexy. Staff and
customers, they all paw at her all the time, but he doesn't care, poor him.
I think he's gay.

EVA

(*to Margareta*) The scarf— be careful—it's a Gucci.

ANN

She's a waitress too. Nineteen years old.

EVA

You're sitting there twisting it the whole time—like a dish rag.

MARGARETA

I'm being careful. I love it!

EVA

From New York.

ANN

It's because I'm talking. She doesn't like words like "gay" and "fag,"
whatever she thinks those mean.

MARGARETA

I think this scarf is wonderful, so soft . . . and elegant. It feels so good on my skin . . . It's so . . .

ANN

She acts like she's in a soap opera or something.

EVA

Dad? (*about the wine*)

HENRICK

No, thank you.

MARGARETA

For once, have a glass of wine when others are around.

HENRICK

I'm fine . . . I'm really fine.

MARGARETA

Yes, everything was really quite tasty, if I may say so myself . . . even though the soup curdled. But you don't notice it, if you don't look at it.

HENRICK

Is that why it's so dark in here?

EVA

Do you put the whole peeled avocado in, the way it is, and then let it boil?

MARGARETA

It shouldn't boil—that's the thing.

HENRICK

It's the horse radish . . .

MARGARETA

(*listens*) Quiet. They are out there . . .

HENRICK

. . . that gives it pizzazz.

MARGARETA

Our neighbors across the hall . . . and then I warmed the quiche, for Ann, and made a special sauce for her.

ANN

You don't have to go over everything you've been doing. We've been here the whole time.

MARGARETA

Because I remember how she hates cold food . . . in a little melted butter and some lemon.

ANN

I LOVE cold food, but not when it's cold outside! I love cold food! But not in the end of October! In July cold food can be very refreshing.

MARGARETA

One can hear every little sound from out there.

HENRICK

It was the floor that squeaked.

MARGARETA

The other day she told me that she goes to the gym every Monday.

EVA

I really don't eat right.

HENRICK

Who?

MARGARETA

Our neighbor's wife. So, then the children are left alone. (*to eva*) That's what happens.

HENRICK

You shouldn't let it happen.

MARGARETA

But you're such a good cook.

ANN

I have to make sure that John gets good, healthy food.

EVA

It seems that all I've got time for is a leftover hamburger.

ANN

He has to have a good home-cooked meal every night. But now he's getting fat again.

MARGARETA

(*to Eva*) That's not good.

ANN

He's inherited his dad's slow metabolism.

EVA

As a reward? Well, there's no time for me to live a normal life . . .

ANN

But you get a lot of money for it.

EVA

I'm happy there, I'm not complaining.

MARGARETA

I always eat dinner with Henrick when he gets home. That's our little moment when we relax together. It's usually very pleasant.

EVA

I really don't like wine that much, but I'm trying to learn to like it.

HENRICK

Usually I get home around 6:30.

ANN

(*to Eva*) You two have as much money as God.

EVA

Oh, well.

ANN

You and Mattias. You have everything there is to buy.

EVA

We have enough money to feel good.

MARGARETA

It's so silly, but he, Henrick, always calls out, no, he never raises his voice . . . but out there in the hallway he says: Hello, it's me. . . . I'm home. Who else could it be, I'd like to know? By that time I want everything to be ready, so that I can feel calm and relaxed and we can have a little glass of sherry or scotch before dinner.

HENRICK

Margareta always wants a glass of sherry before we eat.

ANN

An unbelievably expensive home, an Alfa Romeo and a BMW.

EVA

You forgot the tractor mower.

ANN

Yes, and a home decorated by top designers, oriental rugs and Biedermeier pieces, and so many clothes you could throw up.

MARGARETA

We really have it very good, Henrick, when you think about it. Am I right? (*little pause*) Yes, we do. I'll answer myself. Finally I've reached the point when I'll become a real recluse, fixed in my views about everything, and not worry about what other people think, and stop trying to live up to the role of happy mother and wife. I'll be satisfied if I can stay healthy and if I can spend time in the country for the rest of my life—walk alone on the beach and turn over rocks. I deserve that. I had a little to do with it too . . .

EVA

What? Mom.

MARGARETA

That we've been blessed with such good and smart children.

EVA

Well, yes.

ANN

Good and smart?

MARGARETA

Yes, that's what I think, I think both of you are so good and smart. I don't understand how you find time for everything. A home, friends, a challenging job, and then you find the time to come here every week.

EVA

I usually organize my days very carefully.

ANN

Contrary to me.

MARGARETA

We had a little something to do with that, right, Henrick? We instilled good habits in you.

ANN

I usually get my days organized for me.

HENRICK

I'm saying that we gave our girls a safe and harmonious childhood.

ANN

Death is always safe.

MARGARETA

I know that Eva thinks that anyway—that she had a good and harmonious childhood here . . . with us . . . with you and me . . .

ANN

Yea, that's good I guess.

MARGARETA

A healthy, wholesome and athletic family, without quarrels and too many problems, thank God. . . . But athletic, what do you mean by that, Eva?

EVA

Did I say that?

MARGARETA

Were we an athletic family? We used to go for long walks and we swam like other families, but we never did any sports, did we? Henrick? Did you and Eva do something behind my back? Well, you took her to basketball . . . or was it to the ballet . . . or was that with Lena . . . Ann?

EVA

I played golf with Dad.

MARGARETA

No, you weren't really interested, Lena . . . Ann, in anything athletic.

ANN

We had to go to ballet class to get a straight back, a good straight bourgeois back. (*sits up very straight*) A hard, tense back that could push everything away.

MARGARETA

Ballet dancing is a very healthy activity. You do get a straight back, and you do learn how to move gracefully with self control and pliability.

EVA

(*to Ann*) Ugh, that sounds really sad . . .

ANN

So that you would be able to see yourself in us.

MARGARETA

Yeh, yeh. . . . Still, Henrick, you've got two strong, intelligent and independent daughters . . . and rather beautiful too . . . if I may say so myself.

HENRICK

You may.

MARGARETA

And they didn't get it from me!

EVA

Golf, that's my only relaxation.

MARGARETA

Yes, I think Henrick should start playing again, now that he's almost
ready to retire. Then you don't have to be bored here with me. You get
old very fast if you don't stay alert. One has to have things to do.

EVA

On cold, brisk autumn mornings, alone on the green. Wonderful. Now
and then you see a deer . . .

MARGARETA

How cute . . .

EVA

. . . crossing the course.

MARGARETA

But I try to keep up with things. I'm not that old, am I? Am I?

EVA

You've time to breathe.

ANN

You talk as if we were teenagers.

EVA

I'm forty-three. Old. Worn-out.

ANN

I'm thirty-eight . . . just as worn-out.

MARGARETA

And you aren't either, Henrick. You're just as young as when I met you,
only a little more . . . how should I say . . . melancholy . . . or maybe I
mean a little sadder . . . and your hairline is a little higher, I admit, but
otherwise you're almost as youthful as you used to be. And those glasses
Eva gave you make you look much more up to date.

HENRICK

Unless it's my face that's "up to date" again.

MARGARETA

(*confesses*) Still . . . things happen to the body . . . to our state of mind. (*laughs*) In my darkest moments I feel as if this old building is ready for demolition.

ANN

(*to Eva*) You know, you two will always be OK.

EVA

So, don't we have the right to be OK?

ANN

We're the ones going to hell. We're the ones left at the bottom.

HENRICK

Having money isn't easy either.

ANN

For me it would be incredibly easy.

HENRICK

People with a lot of money aren't under the illusion that money solves any real problems—only creates different ones.

EVA

He just went out and bought a Sony video system for thousands of dollars. . . . I think that was a little unnecessary.

ANN

I'd be ashamed. Aren't you ever ashamed?

EVA

No . . . I guess I kind of keep it in perspective.

ANN

What do you mean by that?

MARGARETA

It's so nice to be able to make videos of friends and . . . acquaintances.

ANN

Were you going to say "children"?

EVA

You're allowed.

ANN

How sweet.

MARGARETA

It's so easy to use, it's practical, weighs hardly anything . . .

EVA

But with some people money has almost become part of who they are.

HENRICK

That's really something compared to our old eight millimeter films . . .

ANN

Those I love, I love them . . . our old films where we look like clowns in a mental institution. They're unbelievable. You wave and laugh and jump around like a nut, so that someone will notice you.

EVA

Yes, we can use it for a lot of things. (*smiles*)

HENRICK

Why don't we ever look at them any more?

ANN

(*To Eva*) Oh, yes, aha . . . yes, I know what you mean.

EVA

Yes.

ANN

Yes, one has to come up with stuff to entertain oneself.

HENRICK

I would think that it's mostly that those with money can acquire possessions a little faster than others . . . who may have to wait a few years.

ANN

When you don't care any more if you have it or not.

EVA

Otherwise it's just too boring.

ANN

You've got to run like hell in order to stay where you are.

MARGARETA

Yes, just think of all the VCR's in every home nowadays.

ANN

Not in mine, we don't even have a color TV. John watches everything in black and white.

EVA

But money doesn't make you rich.

ANN

Use your imagination, I always say.

EVA

We practically live the way poor people live. But we work longer hours. We have to have three cars in order to work so much.

MARGARETA

With the kind of education that Eva got, it should pay well, shouldn't it? As hard as you work.

EVA

We live a rather normal life.

ANN

A little while ago you said you DIDN'T have time to live a normal life.

MARGARETA

Well, nothing extravagant anyway.

ANN

Be quiet!

EVA

A life that's normal for people who have it pretty good.

MARGARETA

Your boss couldn't manage one day without you. You take care of
everything. You have to look good and be well-dressed and see to it that
both Mattias and your boss get equal attention. You don't have time to
get sick or tired. You have to look good every single morning.

ANN

Not like me . . .

EVA

That sounds horrible.

MARGARETA

Horrible? That's not what I meant.

ANN

I don't give a damn what you meant.

HENRICK

Ann . . .

ANN

Well, what the hell would I do with golf-clothes or Gucci bags when I'm
a waitress in a fag restaurant downtown?

HENRICK

Ann. Ann. Ann.

MARGARETA

My impression is that people like that have a very good feeling for
womanly elegance . . . but maybe it's different where you are. But if you
buy classical styles with good quality, then . . .

ANN

. . . you can be as fascistic as you like.

MARGARETA

No, you save money in the long run. I've never tried to save money by
not buying good quality. Then I'd rather not get any . . .

ANN

Solidarity.

MARGARETA

Any extras—entertainment and . . . travel. We've never spent much money on entertainment, and we've never traveled very far, Henrick and I.

ANN

All I'm asking is to live a little bit above the minimum.

HENRICK

I remember a trip to Italy.

MARGARETA

I don't.

HENRICK

Really.

MARGARETA

How nice for you.

HENRICK

Of course you remember . . .

ANN

I would like not to worry every goddamned second about how we're going to manage. And I wouldn't mind not living in our one room apartment downtown, for John's sake.

MARGARETA

Yes, I understand, I understand.

HENRICK

Yes, of course.

EVA

You know, I can drive you home if you want.

ANN

I can't even find room for my dishes there.

MARGARETA

Still, I always tried to keep you two girls well-dressed and neat.

ANN

My God, how she goes on and on about things.

HENRICK

Look who's talking.

ANN

(*to Henrick*) You always take her side. . . . Don't you have spine, any guts!

EVA

(*lightly*) Don't talk to my Dad like that.

MARGARETA

And you looked so adorable and cute together.

ANN

Like little "Hitler "*jugend,*" or whatever it's called.

MARGARETA

You looked wonderful.

ANN

Oh my God, how I hated those ugly, dark green school uniforms and all those black and blue loden coats you made us wear.

MARGARETA

(*to Ann*) Oh, look at your cigarette, take it, take it, so it doesn't make a stain on the tablecloth.

ANN

Ugh . . . I get itchy just thinking about it.

MARGARETA

I thought those coats were wonderful.

ANN

I was ashamed in school because I felt so fake, so deformed. It wasn't me. . . . I definitely didn't like to walk around like a copy of Eva . . . in the same kind of clothes . . . as if there was no difference between us. There was a damn big difference between us.

MARGARETA

I thought you looked so lovely in your clothes.

HENRICK

I'm wearing the same suits I wore in the fifties.

ANN

It made my whole childhood sad and gloomy. That too.

MARGARETA

Really. That's very sad to hear, very sad to hear. (*makes a motion to stand up, starts to take the plates*) Do you want to stay here?

EVA

Do we have a choice?

HENRICK

Life is hard.

ANN

(*to Henrick*) You and your clichés—that's your occupational hazard. Sherry and clichés.

HENRICK

Margareta is the one who likes sherry.

MARGARETA

I never heard Eva complain.

ANN

She never did complain.

EVA

So, we're back to that again, that people like to dress well and expensively.

MARGARETA

What kind of clothes would you have liked then?

ANN

In order for the rich to look very rich and for servants to look like servants.

MARGARETA

Boys' over-alls?

EVA

Nowadays there's no real underclass.

ANN

No, only unreal. I wanted to go naked. I thought my beautiful brown eyes were enough.

HENRICK

Are your eyes brown?

ANN

Sometimes brown, sometimes green.

MARGARETA

But I guess everybody has the possibility to develop the talents they were given . . . I guess that's what this whole societal development has been all about, but I guess I've only experienced it from a distance.

HENRICK

I don't think one can tell any more what segment of society people come from.

ANN

No, isn't that horrifying!

HENRICK

No, on the contrary.

ANN

I think you two should make a trip out to one of those suburbs where I was forced to live the first couple of years after John was born, then you'll see. I was lucky when I was growing up—my generation is probably the last one to live with the same naïve beliefs that you had about the future; that natural resources would never cease . . . now the young ones know what to expect. . . . Also, what really frightens me are these young rich people who've surfaced these last couple of years. They lack both God and ideology; they have no ties to anything outside of themselves. Soon they'll be ruling the rest of us, and then we'll have a society as hard and cold as in the USA. . . . Over there all human considerations have been pushed aside by capitalistic bulldozers.

EVA

(*feels one of her molars with her tongue*) I have a dentist appointment tomorrow.

MARGARETA

Well, now I think we'll move into the living room.

ANN

(*sighs*) God . . . Dad . . .

EVA

Well . . . It would be strange if I don't have any new cavities after having been in America . . . all that Coca Cola.

ANN

Dad?

HENRICK

What?

ANN

Nothing . . . she vanished. (*means Margareta,who went into the kitchen*)

EVA

You get hooked . . . Coca Cola dependent. (*picks up a chair, wants to put it somewhere*)

ANN

(*to Henrick*) How are you? How do you feel?

HENRICK

I'm fine.

EVA

(*about the chair*) Where does it go?

ANN

Nowhere. It showed up by itself.

HENRICK

On caffeine, yes. I'll take it.

ANN

You look really very tired . . . tired and unhappy.

EVA

That's right. We kept popping caffeine pills all day long to get through the discussions. I think I swallowed five, six pills every three hours, and I think it helped.

HENRICK

You shouldn't do that!

ANN

Tired and unhappy, I said.

EVA

Well, but what can you do, what to do?

MARGARETA

(*comes back from the kitchen with a big tray, starts to put dishes on it*) What, honey?

EVA

You can't sleep when you're in New York, it's impossible. And you think much faster; I was thinking twice as fast over there.

ANN

Yes, you really ARE terrific.

MARGARETA

(*to Henrick, about some leftovers*) Do you want it? (*pause*) Do you want this?

EVA

Yes, I'm pretty terrific.

MARGARETA

You always were, both of you.

EVA

Dad, do you want this?

HENRICK

There's only one left.

EVA

Take it! (*takes the full ashtray, holds it in front of her, walks through the room over to the desk by the window*) At the opening ceremony of the House of Representatives a member of the Environmental Green Party gave the . . . (*empties the ashtray slowly into the wastebasket by the desk*) opening address.

ANN

I don't think you are what you said you are.

MARGARETA

What time is it?

EVA

A member of the Green Party?

ANN

No, happy. (*to Margareta*) Did you miss your gardening program?

EVA

It depends on what you mean.

ANN

Same thing you do.

EVA

(*walks over to the window by the desk and looks out*) I like to . . .

ANN

I didn't ask you what you like.

EVA

You didn't?

ANN

No.

EVA

But it makes me happy . . . what I do, the things I do . . . to deal with problems, the worse the better, to create some kind of order . . .

HENRICK

Yes, Eva was always very logical, even as a child.

EVA

Logical thinking, analyses, trying to solve real problems—those things give me satisfaction.

ANN

Yes, logic is good, if you want to avoid responsibility.

MARGARETA

Children are logical.

EVA

I feel happy when I look in my calendar and see that I'm fully booked until April next year.

MARGARETA

I don't hear as well as I used to. (*touches her ear*)

EVA

I love to travel to New York. We came in for landing just as the sun was beginning to set. Saw the sunset from beginning to end.

HENRICK

(*to Ann*) I'm feeling great.

ANN

Don't you have any guts?

HENRICK

No, I don't. No guts but I'm feeling great!

ANN

(*to Eva*) Do you happen to have some condoms with you?

EVA

Condoms? For what?

ANN

Don't tell me you don't know what they're used for?

EVA

Why would I carry those things around?

ANN

Sometimes you do . . . because you're going to . . . or at least you'd like
to . . .

EVA

No, not me.

ANN

I was just wondering.

EVA

That's something . . . well, the man should . . . well, you know.

ANN

You don't think he'd dare to buy condoms, do you. He goes to Iraq, but
he wouldn't dare to buy condoms. I'd fucking better get them, if I want
something to happen.

EVA

Him? Peter again? Are you meeting up with him later?

ANN

I guess I will. What am I to do? I don't know what I do more of,
waitressing or masturbating. Don't tell them, though. Promise.

EVA

Why would I tell them?

ANN

I guess I better do it now, while he's taking care of our child.

HENRICK

Should I get some more wine?

MARGARETA

I thought we would have a little port wine with the fruit.

HENRICK

Yes, of course.

MARGARETA

Don't tell me you forgot to buy port wine?

HENRICK

No, I didn't say that.

MARGARETA

You didn't open it, did you? (*Henrick comes back from the kitchen.*) (*about Ann*) I think she's quite nice tonight. I haven't seen her this pleasant in a long while. (*calls out*) The fruit, Henrick!

HENRICK

So, that's it then.

MARGARETA

The fruit! You forgot the fruit! What are we going to have with your p port wine?

ANN

Don't shout. I'll get it.

MARGARETA

I'm not shouting.

ANN

What goddam fruit are you talking about?

MARGARETA

He only remembered the port wine.

EVA

(*facing Henrick*) Hello, shall we dance?

MARGARETA

You don't know how to serve the fruit.

ANN

What, I don't know how to serve . . . Hell, I know what to do with a few fucking pieces of fruit. (*Ann and Margareta go out to the kitchen.*)

EVA

Do you think . . .

HENRICK

I guess it's like this in most families. What, my friend? (*He opens the bottle.*)

EVA

Well, I was wondering if I could ask you to call in a prescription for some pills for me?

HENRICK

Pills? What kind of pills?

EVA

At some drugstore . . . There must be a couple of them open this late.

HENRICK

Are you sick? Pills?

EVA

No, but I can't sleep. I need something to help me sleep. Something. Valium, anything . . . Demerol.

HENRICK

Demerol?

EVA

Yes, so that I'll sleep.

HENRICK

Do you really need it?

EVA

Of course I need to sleep. Everybody needs to sleep. (*short pause*) I shouldn't have asked you.

HENRICK

Well, yes, but . . . to take pills . . .

EVA

What about it?

HENRICK

I don't think that's good.

EVA

Good? Is it better to anesthetize oneself with alcohol instead? I can't seem to unwind. There are too many things spinning around. It's too much!

HENRICK

Yes, yes, I can understand that.

EVA

I feel like I'm getting sick. I only get three or four hours of sleep at night.

HENRICK

I seem to remember I prescribed Demerol for you during the summer.

EVA

I don't think so. Besides, I only use it when I need to!

HENRICK

Yes, it can become a dangerous habit.

EVA

(*suddenly aggressive*) What the hell is wrong with you! Are you saying that I'm dependant on them! Addicted . . .

HENRICK

No, no.

EVA

Do you think I'll become addicted?

HENRICK

Of course I can write out a prescription for you, but I feel I have to tell you . . .

EVA

Forget it! I'll ask someone else! I don't need you to be suspicious of me, just because I have a little problem adjusting from one part of the world to another.

HENRICK

But Eva . . . I get worried . . .

EVA

Forget it! I'll manage.

HENRICK

Eva . . . What's the matter?

EVA

God . . . my God!

ANN

(*comes in to the room with the fruit*) What's going on? Everybody calling for God.

EVA

I'm the only one calling for God.

ANN

Anything going on?

HENRICK

No, nothing.

ANN

Are you sure? (*walks over to the table, puts down the fruit plate*) Well, well. (*sits down*) Did you look in the refrigerator? "Repulsion," decay. God, how I hate to come here.

HENRICK

You do?

ANN

Yes, I don't know why I come here. (*drinks wine*) I come here because I don't want to come here. By the way, I guess there's no chance to ask you for loan, is there, to survive?

EVA

No.

MARGARETA

(*comes in from the kitchen holding a glass*) A loan? No, that's out of the question. Henrick!

ANN

No, you only give loans to people who already have money.

HENRICK

Eva doesn't work in the loan department.

EVA

I'm just a glorious-looking neurotic secretary.

MARGARETA

Just a secretary. You, who take care of everything . . .

ANN

Well, I don't have a chance here. So . . . today I did what other bag-ladies do, I didn't see any other solution. . . . I went down to the Salvation Army and begged, and I got seventy-five bucks.

MARGARETA

What are you talking about?

HENRICK

What did you do?

ANN

Don't choke on the port wine.

MARGARETA

What did you do?

HENRICK

But, my God . . . Ann!

MARGARETA

You're joking.

HENRICK

Ann!

ANN

I told them I have a son, I work from morning to night, right now I have
no money, nada, and we can't manage over the weekend. We have no
money for food.

MARGARETA

But Ann . . .

ANN

What?

MARGARETA

How could you?

EVA

I think that's terrific.

ANN

Well, I'm not ashamed, I'm not one fucking bit ashamed. I can't afford
to be ashamed. The opposite really. I'm grateful that there still are some
caring, generous human beings on this earth.

MARGARETA

My God. You can't walk around begging.

ANN

No, of course it isn't the thing to do in your circles . . . but I have a son
who needs food every day, and he needs a bus ticket because he can't
walk all the way to school now that it's getting cold, and his shoes are
bad too.

HENRICK

Why don't you come to us?

MARGARETA

Yes.

ANN

And where are you?

HENRICK

Why don't you ask us, when you are in trouble?

MARGARETA

Dad can write out a check for you. I've got a whole freezer full of food! But you always refuse to accept our help.

ANN

Thank you very much. You were going to give me some old, black Persian lamb coat from the forties that had belonged to my grandma.

MARGARETA

You could do something with it, if you wanted to!

ANN

And what could I do with some old moose steaks when I only have two hotplates? It's absurd.

MARGARETA

We can't force you.

ANN

But you wish you could.

HENRICK

You know that you can always turn to us if you're in a real bind. What are parents for?

ANN

Yes, I wonder about that too.

EVA

I'm here for you too.

ANN

Well, thank you, thank you.

MARGARETA

Money for a bus ticket we should at least be allowed to give to our grandson.

ANN

Well, do whatever you want to do . . . but I'm fucking tired of hearing how much you've given me already.

MARGARETA

Now you're really silly . . .

ANN

You all manage to make everything my fault.

MARGARETA

. . . and unfair.

ANN

I'll never ever ask for your help. (*short pause*) I may ask for a lot of other things, but not for help.

HENRICK

Why are you talking like that?

MARGARETA

It sounds so unpleasant.

ANN

She wants me to accept things I don't need, a fur coat, old, dirty jewelry, and stuff like that, and then I'm supposed to be grateful for the rest of my life.

HENRICK

How much do you need? (*pause*) Right now? Seventy-five wouldn't be enough, would it?

ANN

I scrimp and pinch on everything. I haven't bought any new clothes for John in two years. He gets stuff from his buddies. I've been to Social Services three times this year already.

MARGARETA

And what do they say?

ANN

(*to Eva*) God . . . She doesn't live in this world.

EVA

My God!

MARGARETA

Couldn't you try to get a better job, so you wouldn't have to have it like this?

EVA

There are plenty of jobs out there right now.

HENRICK

Good jobs.

EVA

Good jobs that are poorly paid.

ANN

I have a real job! I'm a waitress! I work nine hours every day . . .

MARGARETA

Obviously that's not enough if you have to go to the City Mission like a . . . beggar . . . a person in need.

ANN

I have to have a job like this one, otherwise I'd be too late for picking up John! Sometimes I have to bring him with me to the restaurant, when I work late . . . and I also have to find time to write in the evenings. I have no choice, no alternative! NOT ME! There are people with alternatives, but not me! DON'T YOU UNDERSTAND THAT!

HENRICK

But Ann . . . Ann . . .

ANN

DON'T YOU UNDERSTAND ANYTHING . . . .FUCKING IDIOTS!

EVA

Don't shout.

ANN

Goddamn idiots! (pause) Sorry, but . . . I get so fucking angry . . .

HENRICK

We noticed.

EVA

Are you writing?

MARGARETA

Yes.

EVA

What?

MARGARETA

A play. She's writing plays these days.

EVA

Really . . . that's great.

HENRICK

What?

ANN

What . . . just a little fucking play for radio.

EVA

What is it about?

ANN

I would've had it done a long time ago if I didn't have to deal with all this shit. I have a lot to learn, but I know I can be good. One day I'll become a good writer, a damn good writer. Anyway, there are some who believe in me.

HENRICK

I'd like to read it. May I?

ANN

Right now it's just a painful mess. . . . You'll have to wait. You'll have to listen to it when it's on the radio like everybody else.

HENRICK

My rear is getting sore sitting here.

ANN

Don't sit there then.

EVA

Find a comfortable chair.

ANN

He doesn't dare.

MARGARETA

Being comfortable is dangerous. It frightens him.

ANN

I don't even have money for writing paper. I write on the backs of old stuff.

EVA

Dad, you sit like you're waiting for a patient.

MARGARETA

What is it about? (*pause*)

HENRICK

Yes, tell us!

ANN

About you.

MARGARETA

About me? How nice. . . . Is it a comedy?

ANN

Don't be too sure about that. No, it's about . . . memories, fantasies, dreams . . . I don't know.

HENRICK

Tell us, tell us . . .

MARGARETA

Yes.

ANN

Well . . . it's about a man in his sixties, who's rather miserable . . .

HENRICK

Old . . .

ANN

. . . and helpless in life, married to a sadistic woman who can't love her husband, who can't love anyone but herself, and maybe not herself either . . . and who especially can't love her . . .

MARGARETA

Daughters.

ANN

Yes, that's right. How did you know?

MARGARETA

I think I've already seen it—many times . . .

ANN

I've never made myself out to be innovative. I am going to write. I really want to write, damn it . . . if only I could get a couple of hours in every day. I'm a talented person.

MARGARETA

It sounds very exciting.

HENRICK

Very interesting.

ANN

Yes, you bet your ass it is.

MARGARETA

Yes, a lot of fun.

HENRICK

How about some coffee?

EVA

Why not?

MARGARETA

Yes, please.

EVA

(*after a short pause*) Look how dark it is. (*short pause*) But I bring a lot of sunshine to our lives, I think.

ANN

I haven't been feeling so good this last week.

MARGARETA

You haven't?

HENRICK

Really?

EVA

Yes, it isn't easy being Ann.

MARGARETA

Yes, me too.

EVA

So, what kind of medicine would help—Valium?

ANN

No, my head feels strange, I almost fainted a couple of times.

HENRICK

How are your blood counts?

ANN

I don't have any.

HENRICK

What?

MARGARETA

To me you look very healthy and good.

EVA

Well, there's something different.

MARGARETA

Yes, your face looks different.

EVA

Yes, it does.

ANN

It's my hair. (*to Eva*) All of you are so mean!

MARGARETA

You're changing your hair style so often I can't keep up.

EVA

We're just making fun of you.

ANN

Why are you so fucking mean to me, all of you?

HENRICK

Maybe you should take something to build up your immune system?

MARGARETA

So, how do you feel right now, my dear?

ANN

What?

MARGARETA

I'm talking to you, Ann.

ANN

Really.

MARGARETA

Yes. You said that you hadn't been feeling very well.

ANN

Really. No, I don't feel very well. Quite honestly, I'm in a sad state. I almost fainted a few times. I even called the "Sickness Hotline" and described the symptoms and they said it sounded like "Melies" syndrome.

MARGARETA

Really? How strange.

HENRICK

Menieres.

ANN

That's not strange at all. (*to Henrick*) I tried calling you, but no one
answered.

EVA

What is it?

MARGARETA

When?

HENRICK

Where?

EVA

Something serious?

ANN

Some kind of inner ear problem. I looked it up.

HENRICK

Did you faint?

ANN

Yes, I think so. I had to lie down. John got really scared.

HENRICK

I'll take a look at your ear, if you want?

MARGARETA

Aren't you going to have it examined?

HENRICK

I am a doctor.

ANN

I'll see. If I die.

MARGARETA

Ya, ya . . . you get so easily worked up for nothing.

ANN

(*very angrily*) I don't want to hear your stupid, fucking comments any more, they make me sick!

MARGARETA

What?

EVA

Oops.

HENRICK

Your language, Ann . . . Your language!

ANN

She's playing some fucking bullshit game with me, and I don't want to play anymore.

EVA

God . . .

HENRICK

Your choice of words!

ANN

Tell her that!

MARGARETA

My God . . . (*to Henrick*) What's wrong now?

ANN

(*aggressively*) I've been told since I was born . . . that I . . . that I'm hallucinating . . . that I don't feel what I feel. I don't come here to listen to all these fucking insinuations. I come here because you nag and beg, and then I think that I can at least talk to Dad . . . because he doesn't lie, he doesn't know how . . . that's the only reason I come here. I know she doesn't want me here, she only asks because you're supposed to. What's the reason for all of us being here? Well, I know why Eva is here, because one is supposed to keep a nice, indulgent kind of contact with ones parents. . . . And Dad is here because he has to . . . But why am I here?

HENRICK

Enough! Please calm down!

ANN

Why do you want me here? Is there a certain way I should sit to be considered a human being?

HENRICK

Take it easy now.

ANN

I haven't asked for any fucking understanding. I don't want to hear one more time that I'm crazy.

HENRICK

Yeh, yeh, yeh.

ANN

She lies. She's been lying to me my whole life.

MARGARETA

But my dear Ann. (*She stands up, walks over to Ann, who turns away, and sits down next to Ann on the couch. Ann moves away as far as she can get.*) My dear Ann, it wasn't at all the way you heard it.

ANN

This is perverse.

MARGARETA

I meant it as something loving . . . something I remembered . . . how you used to be . . .

ANN

What's she doing?

MARGARETA

The way you reacted when you were a little girl, Ann. My little Ann . . . sweet, dear Ann.

ANN

Yeh, yeh.

MARGARETA

You used to get so excited, so worked up, when you were little . . . like on Christmas . . .

ANN

This isn't Christmas.

MARGARETA

Your whole body would be shaking with expectation. I can still see you standing there in the hallway, your little heart beating . . .

ANN

OK, it's OK, OK.

HENRICK

Listen to your mother.

EVA

Yes, listen!

ANN

OK, OK.

MARGARETA

It was so touching. (*pause*) THAT'S what I was thinking about . . . it wasn't a criticism.

ANN

But my God . . .

MARGARETA

Was that so strange?

ANN

Aha, yes, yes.

MARGARETA

You're very sensitive.

ANN

Sensitive? Yes. God knows I'm sensitive. John is too.

MARGARETA

That's natural when you're a child.

EVA

It goes with the territory.

MARGARETA

That's how it is.

EVA

So, what was I like?

MARGARETA

Yes, what were you like? Much calmer.

ANN

I guess I never knew if I'd ever get anything. Nothing that I wanted, anyway. It was fucking torture, like it is now. (*pause*) And as a matter of fact it has been determined that I had a heart neurosis when I was growing up. I had a sensitive heart, whatever you fucking say, a neurotic heart, a fucking sensitive neurotic heart.

MARGARETA

But Ann . . .

HENRICK

Do you have to use such language?

ANN

Not a psychological neurosis, but a physical pain that affected my heart.

MARGARETA

(*stands up*) Yes . . . yes, maybe that's what it was.

ANN

And it's not that fucking unusual . . .

MARGARETA

Why are you so angry?

ANN

You can feel real panic if no one believes you . . . you feel terrified.

HENRICK

That's something that can happen while growing up.

EVA

Some kind of growth irregularity.

HENRICK

Well, I'm not an expert on the heart.

ANN

The requirements of the heart . . . no, that's for fucking sure.

HENRICK

The illnesses of the heart.

MARGARETA

The anatomy.

HENRICK

Illnesses. Nothing more than common knowledge.

ANN

You can ask Berit if you don't believe me.

MARGARETA

What did you say?

ANN

You can ask Berit if you don't believe me.

MARGARETA

Berit? Berit? Who's that?

ANN

Berit . . . She can tell you I felt terribly sick from all this.

MARGARETA

Berit? Berit?

ANN

From being here . . . because she was the one who took care of me when nobody else . . .

MARGARETA

What about Berit? Who is she? Henrick?

HENRICK

Mm . . . Uhm.

ANN

She took care of me when nobody else did.

HENRICK

Berit!

MARGARETA

Berit? (*pause*) Oh, you mean Berit!

ANN

You know very well who I mean!

MARGARETA

Oh, Berit. Do you mean Berit?

ANN

Who took care of me during my whole horrible childhood.

MARGARETA

You're thinking of that . . . You mean that . . .

ANN

That wonderful warm-hearted girl, who was the only one who showed simple, human humanity.

MARGARETA

That big, morose girl from the North, Henrick.

ANN

Goodness . . . goodness . . . goodness . . . goodness . . .

HENRICK

Yes, yes. Are you stuck?

ANN

If you know what that means . . .

HENRICK

You know, now you're really stuck . . .

ANN

. . . and who protected me from . . .

MARGARETA

Do you remember her, Henrick? A very dark, big and clumsy girl. Our sullen Berit with the big cocker-spaniel eyes. . . . Of course!

ANN

If she hadn't been there for me, I don't know how I would've managed.

MARGARETA

Yes, she was very kind, shy and kind, and very awkward.

EVA

Berit?

ANN

She realized, beyond a doubt, that I was growing up in hell . . . with a mother who was trying to kill me and who chased me around the dining room table . . . with a knife.

MARGARETA

What are you talking about? (*laughs*)

HENRICK

Oh, my . . .

ANN

Because Dad obviously showed her that he preferred me intellectually.

MARGARETA

(*to Eva*) I don't think that you remember her. We hired her when Ann was just born.

ANN

Because you couldn't deal with one more child, especially not someone like me.

MARGARETA

Do you really mean that at five you were a greater intellectual stimulation for Henrick than his own wife?

ANN

Face it, face it . . .

HENRICK

Don't fight!

ANN

Face it, face it . . . before it's too late!

MARGARETA

(*to Eva*) That must've been when I went back to work at the library. You were in school . . .

ANN

Face it!

EVA

Aha! I can't take any more of this conversation. What time is it?

MARGARETA

Yes, what time is it?

HENRICK

It's seven . . . already.

MARGARETA

It wasn't always easy to teach the help where to draw the line, so to speak, to teach them what was only meant for the family. She had no understanding of that, that Berit. I always had to tell her to close the door to her room. Always.

ANN

She's the one I have to thank that I'm not locked up in a mental institution at this point in my life . . .

MARGARETA

Well, perhaps now we could talk about something else?

HENRICK

Yes . . . This doesn't lead anywhere.

EVA

No.

ANN

No, it leads to the truth.

HENRICK

What's the location of that restaurant where you work?

MARGARETA

We really don't get together that often.

HENRICK

No.

ANN

Thank God.

EVA

(*to Margareta*) Your hair-cut looks good.

MARGARETA

You think so? Yes, I think it makes me look a little younger anyway.

EVA

You'll always look young. It's your bone structure. It's all about the bone structure.

MARGARETA

Yes, you're right!

EVA

You have a beautiful cranium.

MARGARETA

Oh, that's a terrible thing to say! I'm not dead yet.

EVA

No, Mom, you look wonderful. Your cranium doesn't let you look old and tired.

ANN

What bullshit!

HENRICK

Yes, that's what I think too.

EVA

You're looking more and more like Katherine Hepburn.

MARGARETA

She's such an intelligent and witty woman.

ANN

And dead.

EVA

Dad is getting a little fat; he's getting a little tummy.

ANN

Not everyone has a biological mother younger than her daughters.

MARGARETA

(*to Henrick*) Ask Ann if she wants some more port wine.

HENRICK

Ann, do you want some more port wine?

ANN

Well, why not?

EVA

I don't like it.

ANN

I'm supposed to be on a diet . . . but, yes please.

MARGARETA

Diet?

HENRICK

Do you really need to be on a diet?

ANN

I get fat very easily. It has to do with emotions.

MARGARETA

But . . . You've always been so thin.

ANN

I've always had a problem.

MARGARETA

But you're just like me and Eva.

ANN

I was a little fatso.

MARGARETA

No, now I really have to protest.

HENRICK

Here you are, Ann.

ANN

I was a real little piglet.

MARGARETA

You were not.

ANN

(*very friendly*) Yes, I was. Fat like a pig. At school they called me fatso.

MARGARETA

You, who never ate anything? How could you be fat? Henrick?

HENRICK

Yes . . .

ANN

At home, no . . . but I ate like crazy at my friends' homes. French fries, fish sticks with tartar sauce—lots of bad, unhealthy foods.

MARGARETA

You were terribly anorexic during those years . . .

ANN

That's what I liked . . . junk food, garbage.

MARGARETA

. . . if I remember correctly.

HENRICK

Well, I don't remember.

EVA

No, she wasn't.

HENRICK

So, I was neither right nor wrong.

MARGARETA

(*to Henrick, rather aggressively*) No, you don't remember anything, do you! You never took part in this family!

EVA

It was me. I was the one who was anorexic. For a short while.

MARGARETA

Maybe once in a blue moon you'd take the girls for a Sunday walk! Not very often!

HENRICK

Really.

MARGARETA

Still, I was the one who went to her . . . Ann's dialyst . . . analyst, I mean.

EVA

This is wonderful . . . Freud all the way.

MARGARETA

Yes, you better believe I did.

ANN

(*amused*) Yes you did, but you kept yourself far away from everything that came up. (*imitates Margareta*) "Oh, what a lovely woman," she said.

MARGARETA

Anyway, I did it. I did it . . . God knows why. Because you asked me. I went with you. Give me some credit for that.

ANN

Well, anyway, I was a real little fatso. Look at those photographs over there on the bureau.

EVA

Breakfront.

ANN

Yes. Where you keep the photos of your little girls.

MARGARETA

You're supposed to be a little plump when you're a child.

EVA

The beautiful one over there, that's me.

ANN

I was fat all the way into my teens. (*puts the photograph in front of Margareta*) Look.

HENRICK

May I have a look?

ANN

That's me, right? A fat girl with bad skin.

MARGARETA

A little plump maybe, but that's only cute. (*about another photograph*) This must be one that Dad took . . . one of those rare times he paid us a visit.

HENRICK

Why don't you stop!

MARGARETA

Sorry.

HENRICK

Please hand me the picture!

EVA

Oops . . .

HENRICK

(*to ease the tension*) Yes, *pardonez-moi*, may I have a look?

MARGARETA

(*as if she didn't hear*) You were sunning yourself on the terrace. That's when Dad took that picture.

EVA

Look, my hair was short there.

ANN

What a little piglet I was.

HENRICK

Photography was my hobby then.

MARGARETA

No, you weren't, you were so cute, so adorable, so cuddly. (*pretends to kiss the photgraph*) No, you were so wonderful, so good and kind and . . .

EVA

My skin never broke out all those years in my teens. Never. My skin was clear and clean. I had wonderful, lovely skin, like marble.

HENRICK

You shouldn't say things like that about yourself.

EVA

Why not, since it's true.

MARGARETA

I think I remember that weekend when you took that picture. You really didn't show much interest in your children. You weren't even there for her birth.

HENRICK

I couldn't help that.

MARGARETA

I guess I didn't want you there either. (*to Ann*) You happened to want to enter this world two weeks early, Ann.

ANN

Doesn't surprise me. (*drops a pile of photographs*)

MARGARETA

Careful with the photographs! I really treasure them.

EVA

I don't have any.

MARGARETA

I'm sure you've got loads of them.

EVA

None.

MARGARETA

From your wedding, from trips and parties.

EVA

Those don't count.

MARGARETA

No?

HENRICK

At that time I worked as an intern. I worked sixteen hours a day. At the Karolinska Hospital, the Thorax Clinic. Never a day off.

MARGARETA

That was when Eva was born. I was so much in love then.

HENRICK

Not even on Good Friday.

MARGARETA

That was when you were charming and funny, God knows. I fell in love instantly. It was as if I'd been hit by lightning when I first saw you.

ANN

Where did you see him?

MARGARETA

He was a combination of bravado and bewilderment.

EVA

Where did that go?

MARGARETA

I admired him. He was going to be a doctor. He was intelligent. He was kind. He was funny. Not very difficult to like you then, honey. (*to Ann and Eva*) He was a man that women adored!

EVA

L'homme a 'femme.

MARGARETA

But he was hardly ever home, he had no time for his family . . . for you. But that's the way men were at that time.

HENRICK

I worked from seven in the morning to twelve at night. Those were hard days for a young intern. One walked around in ones sleep.

EVA

One married in ones sleep too.

MARGARETA

He was so boyish . . .

EVA

Like a . . .

ANN

How can you talk like that about someone who's sitting here . . . it's fucking . . .

EVA

Daddy.

MARGARETA

I'm talking about how he used to be! Not about this Henrick sitting here.

HENRICK

Is the difference that big?

EVA

Que sera, sera . . .

MARGARETA

Yes, it is. For me.

HENRICK

Really . . .

MARGARETA

Yes.

HENRICK

That's not good.

MARGARETA

I don't think so either.

ANN

Hell, this is really serious.

MARGARETA

He left me completely alone to take care of all of this. At that time I was a happy, young woman with very different expectations of life. And sure . . . we were happy for a couple of years . . . but then, then . . .

ANN

Then?

MARGARETA

Then. . . . Life never turns out the way you think it should, the way you dream about it, when you're young and naïve.

                            EVA

No, you can't have everything in life.

                            ANN

Really? Tell me about it!

                            EVA

What happened?

                            ANN

What really happened?

                          HENRICK

Nothing. Nothing at all.

                            EVA

It sounds somewhat thrilling.

                          HENRICK

Nothing, I said.

                            ANN

What really happened?

                          HENRICK

It's the way life goes.

                         MARGARETA

It just happens.

                            EVA

Que sera, sera . . .

                         MARGARETA

It was so long ago.

                            ANN

Exactly!

                          HENRICK

There are things that only concern Margareta and myself and nobody
else.

MARGARETA

And whatever it was, it seems so unreal at this time.

HENRICK

Still, we've had it good. Better than most.

EVA

Things are what they are . . .

ANN

Hell no, this doesn't only concern the two of you! There's nothing that happened when I was little that doesn't concern me, since I know that I was pulled into it, and exploited, and I'm so fucking sick because nothing ever gets sorted out.

EVA

Yeh, yeh, yeh, yeh . . .

ANN

I've never been told the truth! It's not so strange that I think that people always lie to me. I'm not stupid! I have a good brain. I'm not stupid in my heart either, I'm not. I want to be free.

EVA

Freedom for you is when you decide everything.

HENRICK

No, no . . . nobody said that you're stupid.

ANN

I want to know what happened. I want to know why I have to feel so fucking bad all the time. Dad, what really happened?

HENRICK

I don't know what you're talking about!

ANN

Yes, you do!

HENRICK

No!

ANN

I know you do!

MARGARETA

I'm sure there are many reasons why you feel bad sometimes. It's not only Dad's and my fault.

ANN

I didn't say that!

MARGARETA

I get so tired of all this digging into our feelings. To constantly be digging instead of trying hard . . .

ANN

You have no feelings!

HENRICK

We've been ordinary, decent parents, who've tried to do our best.

MARGARETA

And we had no more problems than most people.

HENRICK

Probably fewer. . . . Decent financial situation, a nice home and healthy, harmonious children.

MARGARETA

Yes, well, that's how it was then, anyway.

HENRICK

Yes, almost never sick.

MARGARETA

Now I don't want to sit here and discuss this any longer. I refuse, I refuse, I said.

EVA

I hate . . .

HENRICK

There's nothing to talk about!

ANN

(*with a calm threat*) What did you do to me, really! You two, together, or one at a time . . . with me? Can you tell me that?

MARGARETA

Our greatest concern, here on this earth, has been caring for the two of you.

HENRICK

Like it is for most parents. I can't remember that I ever had any big conflict with Margareta.

ANN

But that was a conflict for me . . . that you didn't have a conflict with her!

HENRICK

Really . . .

EVA

Concern for us?

ANN

(*to Henrick*) Did you meet another woman? Did you have mistresses? That I could understand.

HENRICK

(*to Margareta*) Let it be.

MARGARETA

(*to Eva*) Concern for Ann, I meant . . . her poor financial situation and her strange relationships with different men. And whatever else . . .

ANN

Or did you touch me or something? (*pause*) Did you touch me in an inappropriate way?

EVA

(*like a rap from a whip*) OK!

ANN

What?

EVA

Shut up!

ANN

In some way?

EVA

Shut up! Shut up! Keep your goddamn mouth shut!

ANN

What? . . . Did you?

EVA

Ann, go to hell!

ANN

Dad. Say something.

MARGARETA

What are you saying?

ANN

I'm asking.

HENRICK

What are you talking about?

EVA

(*grabs Ann's arm*) Now you've definitely gone too far!

MARGARETA

I don't understand anything.

HENRICK

Touched you? How?

MARGARETA

Hit you? We never hit you.

HENRICK

Hit you?

ANN

In a way that could be misinterpreted. That Mother could misinterpret.

HENRICK

Me—never!

MARGARETA

What are you saying?

ANN

I just want to know.

MARGARETA

This is terrible . . . terrible . . .

ANN

Dad? I just want to know.

EVA

You're a real shit!

MARGARETA

How can you even . . . imply . . .

EVA

You've gone too far . . .

HENRICK

What are you talking about?

ANN

I don't know anything.

EVA

Sick . . . she's sick.

ANN

I'm not sick.

EVA

She's crazy as a loon.

ANN

I'm not crazy.

MARGARETA

She really is.

HENRICK

I don't understand anything.

MARGARETA

Me neither.

ANN

All I know is that I've been violated. I feel fucking violated within.

MARGARETA

You aren't one bit violated! We are the ones who are violated and humiliated. I feel utterly violated. Do you know what you're saying?

ANN

Yes, indeed I do!

MARGARETA

How will I ever be able to forgive you!

ANN

I don't want your forgiveness! Stuff it up your ass, if you want!

MARGARETA

Henrick! Henrick!

HENRICK

Ann, stop it!

ANN

I've always been pulled into your fucking emotional conflicts . . .

MARGARETA

We're leaving.

ANN

You've used me as a tool against one another.

HENRICK

Go to your room, Margareta!

MARGARETA

No, I'm not going to be forced out of my own home.

ANN

I think my very first memories are that she . . . that you're following me trying to hurt me, because Dad liked me so much. . . . But I didn't dare to show that I liked Dad, because then I'd be punished. . . . On the other hand, when things were good between the two of you, then I was supposed to like Dad so very much . . . and show it for Mom, as if she would be praised for it. Do you understand? I didn't feel secure at all, except with Berit, because she was simple and real, and I understood that.

MARGARETA

I don't know if I'll ever be able to forgive you . . . or myself, for letting it go this far.

HENRICK

Those are only fantasies.

ANN

Fantasies . . . That's all I have. I used to have a recurring dream—I still do. I dream I'm on an uninhabited island far out at sea . . . either with you or with mother . . .

HENRICK

Islands usually are out at sea.

ANN

A very tiny island, so tiny that there's room for only two people. All it is, is a dead rock in the ocean.

MARGARETA

How do you survive out there?

HENRICK

Don't interrupt!

ANN

I'm mostly there with Dad trying to comfort him.

HENRICK

Really? Why?

MARGARETA

It's only a dream . . .

ANN

To get him, you, Dad, to feel happier . . .

MARGARETA

Yes, of course.

ANN

. . . and not so hopeless and just sitting there like you're paralyzed . . .
like now.

MARGARETA

Well, first of all, he isn't sober.

ANN

We've given up all hope of anyone coming to get us. Then this incredible
thing happens, a boat comes, a silly little boat with one person in it.

MARGARETA

He doesn't think his patients are noticing . . .

HENRICK

Quiet please!

ANN

If I'm there with Dad a woman comes, and if, by chance, I'm there with
Mother, it's a man. Never Mother and Dad, always a stranger.

MARGARETA

Of course they notice . . . there are fewer and fewer . . . because they
never return.

ANN

I always hope that Dad and Mom will like the stranger, because that's the only chance I have to get away. Then you two won't need me anymore. It's only a dream. . . . I'm really much smarter sleeping than when I'm awake.

MARGARETA

It's a quiet, unreachable kind of drinking that you can't get to. After nine o'clock, after nine every night.

ANN

(*to herself*) I'd like to start a new life and I don't want to see these people any more . . . and they don't want to see me either . . . but if they refuse to tell me anything . . . that's a question my therapist always asks me . . .

HENRICK

What question?

ANN

About you.

HENRICK

About me?

ANN

Yes, where is he?

HENRICK

I don't understand anything. Can someone please explain it to me?

ANN

Where's Dad? . . . Where are you?

MARGARETA

(*starts to laugh*) Yes, that's a good question, a very good question. She's asking for all of us, your therapist!

ANN

Dad . . .

MARGARETA

He's never known, or had the will to find out. Neither the strength, the will or the courage.

ANN

Dad . . .

HENRICK

I'm here.

EVA

I don't want to be here anymore.

MARGARETA

He's sitting here. He's sitting here not understanding anything. Answer her. She's talking to you. What? You're white as a sheet.

ANN

I've got such a pain in my heart.

EVA

For that you need a heart.

ANN

I'm in such pain. I've got to lie down.

HENRICK

Are you sure?

MARGARETA

(*to Henrick*) You're the doctor. And the father. . . . Care for her.

ANN

I can't stay here. I've got to get away from here.

EVA

Calm down.

HENRICK

That's not where the pain is, if it's the heart.

MARGARETA

She can lie down in my room. I can't do any more for her.

ANN

God, I'm so scared.

HENRICK

(*stands up and walks over to Ann*) Maybe you better lie down for a while in mother's room.

ANN

No.

HENRICK

Ann, dear little Ann.

ANN

No.

MARGARETA

Please get her out of this room!

HENRICK

Yes, yes. (*to Ann*) Come with me now.

EVA

Then I'll drive her home.

MARGARETA

I don't want to see her anymore.

(*Henrick helps Ann to her mother's bedroom. He comes back.*)

EVA

My God, how dramatic.

MARGARETA

I'm sure she can write plays about all kinds of things.

EVA

I wonder how it is for John.

MARGARETA

The same as for us . . . poor boy.

EVA

Someone has to do something!

MARGARETA

Haven't we tried . . . for thirty years!

HENRICK

It only gets worse . . . if you try to step in.

MARGARETA

When did you ever step in!

EVA

It's sick.

HENRICK

I do what I can.

MARGARETA

And ridiculous.

HENRICK

Did you hear what I said? Well, now I think we need a little scotch. What do you say? (*pause*) Margareta?

MARGARETA

I'm not saying anything.

EVA

Should I?

MARGARETA

Yes, drink, drink. (*short pause*) Maybe she'll fall asleep.

EVA

I'll have to leave soon. Mathias thought he'd be home around eleven.

MARGARETA

You have your Mathias, thank God, my darling.

EVA

Yes.

HENRICK

Yes, Mathias. (*He pours whiskey in three glasses, walks over to Eva and*

Margareta with their glasses, then goes back to his chair and sits down.)
He really works a lot, doesn't he?

EVA

He wants us to move.

HENRICK

From the house?

EVA

Into the city. It's easier living here. It has more going for it.

MARGARETA

How long have you been talking about this?

HENRICK

You mean, sell it?

EVA

If it's possible. A little change in a way.

HENRICK

Of course it's possible. It's quite big.

EVA

Horribly big.

MARGARETA

Horribly big?

EVA

At this point in my life, I mean. It's big and dark and dank. Maybe someday it'll burn to the ground. (*pause*) The garden is nice though. With the cherry orchard.

MARGARETA

Yes, it's wonderful. A garden like that—with cherry trees—I'd like that.

EVA

Mom, what's wrong?

HENRICK

I guess the leaves have already turned autumn colors.

EVA

Winter colors. Mom?

HENRICK

Today, though, it was nice and warm.

EVA

No feeling of winter anyway.

HENRICK

Soon enough ice will cover all the lakes.

EVA

A little more like winter. (*pause*) Mom? How do you feel?

MARGARETA

I don't know . . . and I don't care.

EVA

No, just as well.

MARGARETA

I'm starting to think I don't know who I am anymore . . . It's as if she's trying to take away my identity.

HENRICK

You know how she is.

MARGARETA

No, I don't!

HENRICK

Can't we talk about something else?

MARGARETA

Eva, when you go out, where do you go these days? Where do you eat lunch?

EVA

Where I eat?

MARGARETA

Yes, where do you have your lunch?

EVA

There's a little place across from where I work . . .

MARGARETA

How's the food? Is it expensive? (*long pause*) In there, in my bedroom, there's a human being who's filled with hatred and accusations, someone who doesn't know how she can best hurt me.

EVA

Why do you even care?

MARGARETA

She's my child!

EVA

She . . . runs like a truck through everything. . . . She loves it. She loves the attention. She never waits for you to finish even one sentence. Yes, that's right, that's right, she says—I know exactly.

HENRICK

That's when I like her the most, when she's like that . . . so intense . . .

MARGARETA

I feel like I have a big hole in my stomach. As if I'd been cut open. I feel absolutely empty.

EVA

That's terrible.

MARGARETA

Yes . . . yes.

EVA

Why isn't she in therapy?

MARGARETA

She is. She says.

HENRICK

She goes to a therapist.

EVA

Wow.

MARGARETA

It only makes it worse.

HENRICK

Yes. (*pause*) But . . .

MARGARETA

She's thirty-eight years old! She is an adult.

HENRICK

But . . .

MARGARETA

I hate all those silly therapists, who just sit there on the outside making judgments! Didn't we give her enough attention? Or . . .? She blames me for everything that has happened to her. Ann, I mean. I'm the one who's made her sick . . .

HENRICK

Sick?

MARGARETA

I'm not crazy, Henrick. However much I try . . . you know, well, ever since your mother took all my time before Ann started to need me . . . to try to adjust to her unpredictable moods and changes . . . every time we see each other, every time I spend time with her, she looks at me with more hatred in her eyes . . . big deep wells of hatred. I don't know how to behave with her anymore. I can't ignore that she's in pain . . . because then I'd be crazy, and I'm not crazy, that much I know.

HENRICK

I think that that's when you are, when you know that you aren't.

MARGARETA

Yeh, yeh, yeh . . . since you're the expert . . . since you've seen it up close . . . but I know I'm not. As long as Eva seems to be a well-adjusted human being who I can talk to. . . . But if it has to be like this . . . I tried to bring up only general topics at the dinner table . . . global warming, animal rights . . . but, I don't want to be humiliated. Nothing is going to change her mind . . . about how everything has been, since she was OUR little Ann . . . and obviously she wasn't ours either. She was Berit's little Ann . . . another unbelievable insult. Well, well, but I do wonder why you . . . during these forty years . . . when you for some reason did take someone's side, always sided with her, always Ann and never me! Never my side! You've never taken my side! Which is what you should've done!

HENRICK

What? What am I supposed to do now? What side?

MARGARETA

Mine . . . mine or Ann's.

HENRICK

How do you mean?

MARGARETA

Are we supposed to go on like this?

HENRICK

What do you want me to do?

MARGARETA

(*screams*) I want you to choose sides! Make up your mind! Decide what you want, once and for all!

HENRICK

Choose?

MARGARETA

YES!

HENRICK

Choose what?

MARGARETA

Between her and me!

HENRICK

How? This is crazy. How can I choose between you and Ann, my daughter. Margareta!

EVA

Dear little Mom!

HENRICK

We can't . . . deny her.

MARGARETA

Right now I could. Didn't you hear what she said about you . . . what she implied?

HENRICK

She was just confused.

MARGARETA

Yes, and how much confusion do we have to swallow!

HENRICK

Maybe it's silly to keep up these dramatic monthly family gatherings.

MARGARETA

Let's put an end to them, fine with me . . .

EVA

(firmly) I don't want them to end! I like them!

MARGARETA

Why should I have to feel nervous for days just because you two are due here?

EVA

I like coming here!

HENRICK

It's a way for us to still keep in touch with the two of you.

EVA

It's the only thing I have!

HENRICK

Thank you. . . . That was nice of you to say.

EVA

I was happy here with you.

MARGARETA

You were, yes! But she was unhappy for all of us.

EVA

I loved you both . . . just as much then, as I do now. I think it's getting worse. She doesn't do a damn thing to face her situation. She blames everything and everyone just as long as she doesn't have to face anything. You two have to choose . . . somehow. When she's done there isn't much left. . . . I'm thinking of my own life. I can't worry about her life. . . . I don't want my parents treated like some goddamn Kurds.

MARGARETA

I'm so used to it, dear. She stopped going to school by the time she was twelve—just quit. That's when she really needed a father who would've put his foot down. When she was thirteen, I think, she became a "Communist" just to shock people around our neighborhood, but mostly to shock me. . . . Then she moved away from home when she was fourteen and started to live with men at least thirty years older than she was, married, had children . . . survived on rice and tea and cigarettes . . . and now, twenty years later she has the nerve to come back and make us responsible! For what? . . . If I may ask? What did we do!

HENRICK

I did everything I could . I wasn't sure you were right all the time. You can't force . . .

MARGARETA

(*interrupts*) I had to trust my own common sense and my own values! Now you see that I was right!

EVA

(*interrupts*) Ann, Ann, Ann! Only Ann, there's no one like Ann! All we talk about is Ann, Ann and her unbelievable problems and her fucking damn life and who's to blame! . . . She's thirty-seven years old! Don't you think it's time for her to take responsibility for her own life!

MARGARETA

Yes, yes, yes, that's what I'm saying.

EVA

Or are you two going to continue to baby her! Well, do it then! I certainly don't want to talk about her anymore!

MARGARETA

I agree with you!

EVA

She doesn't even take care of her own child!

MARGARETA

I agree with you!

EVA

Maybe I need you too, but damn it, you're fully booked. Maybe there are moments when I too would like to have a mother and a father!

HENRICK

You must know that we are here for you. You know that.

MARGARETA

You know that we've never had any difficulties with each other.

HENRICK

No, never!

EVA

We've never had anything! Anything! I'm only a nice fucking guest . . . who's polite to my own parents . . . worried to death that I'd make you unhappy . . .

MARGARETA

But Eva . . . sweetheart . . .

EVA

Who fucking cares about me? . . . Do you, do you, or even me? I feel like your old age insurance. If things go wrong with Ann at least you can say . . . Eva is OK . . . She'll take care of it . . . Why do you think I tried to systematically starve myself to death those years before I moved away from home? Did you ever ask yourself that? . . . Never? It never bothered you?

MARGARETA

We were . . . we were never worried about you.

HENRICK

Eva!

EVA

It never occurred to you that I was in a lost state of mind? I used to go and sit in the closet when I was unhappy, just so I wouldn't make you worried.

MARGARETA

We never wanted to interfere in your life. . . . Never, Eva.

HENRICK

Never.

EVA

Maybe you should have. Maybe that's what you should've done.

HENRICK

On the contrary. We've always talked about how well-adjusted and harmonious you are.

EVA

Sure.

HENRICK

Terrific at everything you set out to do.

EVA

It's not terribly healthy to be terrific. It puts your life in danger.

MARGARETA

You were never difficult.

HENRICK

No!

EVA

No.

HENRICK

Quiet please.

(*They hear Ann opening a door.*)

MARGARETA

So . . . when is Mathias getting home, did you say?

EVA

Around ten-thirty.

MARGARETA

Well, OK then . . . there's plenty of time.

(*Ann enters*)

HENRICK

Oh, here's Ann.

MARGARETA

How are you feeling, honey?

ANN

I just wanted to tell you that you'll get back every cent you've ever given
to me.

MARGARETA

But dear Ann . . .

HENRICK

Sit down and try to be calm.

ANN

I am calm. I'm very calm. (*walks over to Margareta and throws money on the floor in front of her feet*) Consider it partial payment, if you like.

MARGARETA

(*stands up*) I'm sorry, but I never know if I should react or ignore these outbursts.

ANN

I'm sorry you don't know.

MARGARETA

Yes, what should I do?

HENRICK

(*to Ann*) What do you mean by this?

ANN

I don't mean anything any longer by the way I act. I just act!

HENRICK

You have to excuse me, but I don't think . . .

ANN

(*interrupts him*) I don't think there's anything left here that belongs to me. Of course Dad is mine . . . I'm going to explain to John that it's better for him and his mom if we stop seeing Grandma and Grandpa, since it always turns into shit for everyone. John is a sensitive little boy, who's already on shaky ground . . . just like me.

MARGARETA

I think I'd like some coffee.

EVA

Coffee?

MARGARETA

Anyone else?

ANN

Unbelievable. (*to Henrick*) What?

HENRICK

Nothing.

ANN

What?

HENRICK

I'm not saying anything. (*starts to pick up the money*)

MARGARETA

Leave them! I'm making coffee. You're coming with me. You're coming with me to the kitchen.

HENRICK

I'm going to the bathroom.

MARGARETA

All right, and then you're coming to me in the kitchen. I want you to be with me. I demand that you take my side. In everything. (*leaves*)

ANN

(*She walks over to the table, lights a cigarette, looks around. She sees all the photographs, walks over, starts to look at them, puts some in a little pile, walks over to the fireplace, sits down in front of it, carefully puts the big photograph of when she was three in the fireplace. It starts to burn. She takes it out and holds it in front of her while it burns up.*)

HENRICK

(*back from the bathroom, sees her sitting on the floor, but doesn't know what she's doing*) Ann. (*pause*) Ann. (*pause*) Feeling any better?

ANN

(*after a short pause*) Go to mother now.

HENRICK

I want to know how you're feeling. . . . I can do whatever I want.

ANN

Yes, that's what that dog thinks too . . . you know, the one that drools when the bell rings.

HENRICK

Don't you understand anything? (*pause*) Don't you understand that I'm being torn between two different needs and wants? Mother's and yours, Mother and you—all the time.

ANN

So, what about your needs and wants? You don't have any?

HENRICK

My needs . . . I want you two to be nice to each other. . . . What are you doing?

ANN

Nothing. I'm burning my childhood.

HENRICK

But Ann . . .

ANN

My childhood as a good Samaritan. Only me. I'm not burning any of you. I don't want to be part of this anymore. She'll have to talk about someone else from here on, some fantasy figure, someone she thinks loved her . . .

HENRICK

Please stop what you're doing.

ANN

It's just me.

HENRICK

I don't know what to do.

ANN

You don't? (*pause*) You don't?

HENRICK

No, I don't. . . . Maybe you should talk to a doctor. . . . Do you know someone?

ANN

I know you. You're a doctor. These are just photographs. My soul isn't burning up. (*picks up a new photograph*) My hair is burning. I have my Grandma's hair. My mouth is open, as if to whisper something. . . . What? . . . Now my fat little face, so full of anticipation, is burning up . . . my smile has now become a little pile of ashes. How beautiful. Do I remind you of Grandma?

HENRICK

What? . . . I don't know.

ANN

Do I?

HENRICK

I don't know.

ANN

She was talented. . . . I'm not sick. Maybe I'm desperate. But I'm terribly intelligent.

HENRICK

What else?

ANN

That's enough.

MARGARETA

Henrick! Where are you?

ANN

(*starts to laugh*) Oh God! What now? How can you stand it? (*pause*) Living with her?

HENRICK

Stand what?

ANN

That woman!

MARGARETA

Henrick! Where are you!

ANN

Your wife, you know.

HENRICK

Yes, I'm coming!

ANN

(*collects the ashes*) Do you want them?

HENRICK

Put them somewhere she doesn't see them.

ANN

Well, I'm really terribly intelligent. . . . What good does it do me?

HENRICK

Where's John?

ANN

Why do you ask? He's fine. He's with his dad. He has a dad. (*pause*) Ah, here they are.

(*Eva and Margareta enter the room.*)

MARGARETA

I guess we'll sit in here? (*She starts to set the table. Eva is helping her.*)

ANN

A black apron? How dramatic.

MARGARETA

Yes, isn't it nice?

ANN

I'm not having anything.

EVA

(*to Ann*) Feeling better? Want some coffee?

MARGARETA

Turn up the TV sound a little.

ANN

(*to Henrick*) Are you afraid of me?

HENRICK

It's not on.

MARGARETA

Why would he be afraid?

ANN

(*quietly*) Take your coffee and go to hell.

MARGARETA

No one here is afraid.

ANN

I'm not having any coffee. (*pause*) I'm waiting for Eva. I've been promised a ride home.

HENRICK

How about half a cup?

ANN

(*loudly*) I don't want any coffee.

EVA

She doesn't want any.

HENRICK

Don't shout.

MARGARETA

What's that smell?

ANN

It's me.

MARGARETA

Really.

ANN

It's me who's been burnt up. I've burnt up my childhood. (*pause*)

MARGARETA

I think there's news on TV now.

ANN

Burnt child smells bad.

EVA

Yes, it's nine-thirty.

MARGARETA

That early? I feel like half a lifetime has gone by.

(*pause*)

HENRICK

Do you want to watch the news?

MARGARETA

No, it doesn't matter. (*quietly*) Ya, ya!

(*pause*)

EVA

By the way, I saw Peter the other day.

MARGARETA

Peter? . . . Oh, do you mean Peter?

EVA

At restaurant *Val de French*. That's where I saw him, the other day.

MARGARETA

Ann . . .

HENRICK

Ann . . .

ANN

Yes, what?

MARGARETA

That's supposed to be a very good restaurant.

ANN

Why the hell would I care?

EVA

I don't know. I never have the time to eat there.

MARGARETA

Yes, a very good restaurant.

HENRICK

I always bring my own sandwiches.

MARGARETA

Not because we don't have the money!

HENRICK

No, just because I want thirty minutes to myself every day.

MARGARETA

You can have as many minutes as you like, darling!

EVA

He just passed me by. . . . Strange.

MARGARETA

Yes.

ANN

I don't give a fuck about him.

EVA

It was so obvious . . . that he didn't want me to know he saw me.

ANN

No, he hates us like the plague.

EVA

Peter?

ANN

Yes, why don't you all get together and talk about how horrible Ann is, and how you could try to get her committed somewhere?

MARGARETA

He has no reason to dislike us. Why doesn't he like us?

ANN

He hates you, all of you.

MARGARETA

That I don't understand.

ANN

(*to Margareta*) You most of all.

MARGARETA

Me? Peter?

ANN

Yes, you . . . Peter.

EVA

Did you have to ask?

ANN

He says that you are the sleaziest person there is.

HENRICK

ANN, WHAT THE HELL!!

ANN

Dear parents, I'm only reporting. He thinks she's dangerous, unbalanced and not to be trusted. He won't allow John to spend more than a couple of hours here at a time, in order for him not to be harmed. Well, don't look at me.

MARGARETA

Now I'm turning on the TV. I don't want to hear any more from you, thank you.

ANN

That's because he thinks I'm just like you . . . whatever he means by that.

MARGARETA

Enough, I said.

ANN

"I'm being drawn into your unresolved conflict with her," he says. Well, you know, journalists—men in general, men, who abuse women, that's the way they talk these days, finding dubious explanations for everything. Like what's in gasoline that makes it burn? In my case it would be that I loved to sit in my dad's lap until I was eleven.

MARGARETA

What's so strange about that?

ANN

I'm the gasoline in this case.

MARGARETA

All children sit in their fathers' laps.

ANN

That's not what you said then!

MARGARETA

I never said . . . I always said . . .

EVA

Don't talk to her!

ANN

(to Eva) I know that you hate me! You've always thought I was detestable!

EVA

(quietly) I don't think you're detestable . . . but you're very irritating . . . very, very irritating.

MARGARETA

We don't want to get pulled into your troubles. We feel good that we've tried to be as kind as possible.

HENRICK

In your conflicts.

MARGARETA

You've had the use of our country place as often as you like. You've had the second floor all to yourselves.

HENRICK

You spent almost a whole year out there . . . even though you were only going to be there for a week.

MARGARETA

I really enjoyed your visits with sweet John, and Eva and Mathias. We spent almost every midsummer out there together, and that made me very happy. What more can I do?

ANN

I know. I know.

MARGARETA

Henrick too.

HENRICK

To go fishing with John . . .

EVA

Mom, why should you care?

MARGARETA

Yes, why, why? But I don't understand how ungrateful people can be.

ANN

He was the one who wanted us to stay out there that long. . . . I know the price when you get something for free in this house.

MARGARETA

It's good then that you finally seem to have separated . . . you are separated, aren't you?

ANN

Yes, I hope so.

MARGARETA

Yes . . . for John's sake.

ANN

For my sake. I'm tired of relationships. I'm going to become a meter-maid and a lesbian.

EVA

Oh, that sounds wonderful.

MARGARETA

How long were you and Peter together?

ANN

Never . . . for fifteen years.

EVA

That's a long time.

ANN

Fifteen hard years . . . and now these fights about John, on top of everything.

EVA

Yes, I've been with Mathias for seventeen years.

HENRICK

What kind of fights?

ANN

What kind of fights?

MARGARETA

(*to Eva*) You two haven't had any of those. . . . You've had more normal conflicts. . . . You can't compare . . . we've all had those. . . . They bring you closer.

EVA

Unless they separate.

MARGARETA

Normal conflicts . . . it's not easy living together. There are no easy ways.

ANN

No.

MARGARETA

No.

ANN

They lead straight to hell.

MARGARETA

There are the small things, the small catastrophes . . . that bring people together. Small arguments aren't bad. Otherwise the marriage dies . . . just dies. . . . Then you don't even want to see each other in the bedroom. There has to be . . .

EVA

What?

MARGARETA

There has to be . . . needs.

EVA

Passion.

MARGARETA

Yes. On a different level.

ANN

Well, not in your bedroom, because I guess you haven't slept together for twenty years, right? Have you? (*pause*) Have you slept together during these last twenty years . . . had the strength or wanted to? How do you have sex with Margareta? In what end do you start, I almost said?

EVA

You don't have any real plans to shut up, do you?

ANN

Dad, you used to tell me, when I was twelve or thirteen, that women are filthy, what filthy needs they have . . . You must've meant Mom. That it's really difficult to deal with women.

MARGARETA

Enough, I'm not even here.

HENRICK

I think it's time for you to go home now.

ANN

I thought this was my home. But Dad . . . ALL women aren't like mother.

EVA

We really don't care what you say.

HENRICK

No . . . really. There are limits.

EVA

We couldn't care less about your love life.

MARGARETA

Her what?

ANN

My vagina. It has never provided me with any great happiness, it has always given me problems. I've no time for fucking. I'm a walking sexual time bomb.

EVA

That's important information when you find yourself in the emergency room.

HENRICK

ENOUGH!!!! ENOUGH!!!

ANN

But, I won't live much longer anyway. This is my last evening on earth. Haven't you understood that?

HENRICK

Now you really have to stop!

ANN

I want to say something nice . . . about Mom. She has always been a very good looking woman, she still looks very good—beautiful with classical features . . . extremely fixated on sex . . . you know like . . . sexually unfulfilled, always circling around it . . . the forbidden subject.

MARGARETA

(*to Eva, who's holding her coffee mug as if she tried to get warm*) Do you have a cold or are you just sitting like that?

EVA

No.

ANN

I'm sure it can be very exciting for men . . .

EVA

No, no.

ANN

These boyish girls . . .

EVA

No.

ANN

Sure, you didn't know that? You don't know if they are straight or not. (*pause*) Don't try anything with me, Eva. I know you're lying to them not to make them disappointed. I know you lie about everything, just so that they'll be able to remain in their own little universe, their own little world.

EVA

I do?

ANN

You'd never be able to show them the dark side of the moon about yourself.

EVA

And what is that?

ANN

You've told me that you sleep with Mathias only once a month. Then you go into the bathroom and vomit.

HENRICK

What did you say?

EVA

My problem . . . that old stuff. . . . That's not a problem. Everybody knows about it.

(*pause*)

MARGARETA

Yes, but . . .

EVA

Our . . . what should we call it? . . . Tragedy.

ANN

That's a beautiful word. (*pause*) Oh, you sound really low.

EVA

Yes, I'm sitting low in my chair.

MARGARETA

I think you and Mathias have dealt so well with that . . . situation.

HENRICK

(*to Ann*) Have you been taking pills of some kind?

ANN

Eva is the one taking pills.

EVA

Situation?

ANN

Have you given up . . . totally?

EVA

That's not exactly how I'd put it.

HENRICK

One never does.

EVA

No, one never does.

(*pause*)

MARGARETA

Henrick.

ANN

Make me one too, please.

HENRICK

What the hell! One little scotch isn't the end of the world, is it?

MARGARETA

To you it's your whole world.

(*pause*)

EVA

No, I haven't given up.

HENRICK

No, you mustn't do that.

MARGARETA

Hand me the bottle so we can see how much you're using.

ANN

I know.

EVA

No you don't!

MARGARETA

There's nothing wrong with your . . . there's nothing physically wrong.

EVA

You DON'T know how it feels.

MARGARETA

Not with Mathias either.

EVA

No, there isn't anything wrong with either one of us. I just can't hold on to a child. There's no child that has survived coming out of my body.

MARGARETA

You mustn't talk like that.

HENRICK

No, you mustn't.

EVA

Why not?

ANN

You look good with a bottle in your hand, Dad.

MARGARETA

It sounds so terrible, somehow.

HENRICK

You mustn't think of yourself that way.

EVA

How? (*pause*) Like a tomb.

HENRICK

Yes, so negative, so dark.

ANN

That isn't nice.

EVA

But it's so sad.

ANN

She wants everything to be "so very nice" in her little world. But the "little world" isn't very nice out there.

HENRICK

We aren't talking about you right now.

MARGARETA

For a change.

ANN

I just knew you'd say that.

EVA

Soo . . . what does it matter if I continue like this for seventeen more years? Mathias and I.

MARGARETA

What do you mean by that?

EVA

Well, or maybe I should shoot for one last try somewhere. Since I'm . . .

ANN

Then he'd go under, his whole safe, little world would split in half right there, if you came home with some little, dark-haired kid.

MARGARETA

It's not too late. Don't give up.

EVA

I'm the one who wants a child.

MARGARETA

You mustn't give up.

EVA

He'd be happy if I'm happy.

MARGARETA

One can't ever give up.

EVA

I'm not.

ANN

You two can't go on like this anyway.

MARGARETA

We don't have the final say in the matter.

ANN

You've got to do something soon! With yourself.

EVA

What?

ANN

I think you both sound horrible. (*pause*) My soul becomes ice when I listen to the two of you.

MARGARETA

Please be quiet, Ann.

ANN

We still have freedom of speech in this country.

EVA

You really think so?

MARGARETA

Still, last year you hadn't given up anyway.

EVA

No . . .

MARGARETA

You absolutely must not do that.

ANN

Who has the final say? Who does?

MARGARETA

I was just thinking of the Almighty. The Almighty has the final say.

EVA

Although . . . now I think . . . now it's starting . . .

HENRICK

What?

MARGARETA

What's starting?

EVA

Well, the beginning of the end. . . . A little . . .

MARGARETA

The end?

EVA

Yes, of all this! . . . I'll be forty-three this fall!

MARGARETA

No . . .

ANN

Yes, she will . . . and I'm thirty-eight.

EVA

I'm a mature woman. (*laughs*)

ANN

No more knee-socks . . .

EVA

Oh my God, I'm forty-three.

MARGARETA

But Eva . . .

EVA

In a way I've given up.

MARGARETA

Dearest . . . you can't talk like that.

EVA

Stop it.

ANN

Leave her alone.

MARGARETA

What's wrong, darling?

EVA

Nothing, nothing! Leave me alone. (*pause*) Why don't you ever hear what I'm saying?

MARGARETA

We hear what you're saying.

HENRICK

Yes.

EVA

It won't work. It's over. It's dead.

HENRICK

What's dead?

ANN

Do you mean your marriage?

EVA

My marriage.

ANN

To Mathias.

EVA

I mean everything.

HENRICK

Of course it isn't over.

EVA

No, that would be too good to be true.

ANN

(*to Henrick*) You really don't know a fucking thing, you don't know fuck about your children!

EVA

Why couldn't it be?

MARGARETA

(*to Ann*) Maybe you better go and lie down in your room.

EVA

I guess most marriages come to an end, sooner or later.

ANN

In my room? That's where Dad sleeps these days.

HENRICK

You have a good marriage. A very good marriage.

EVA

Really.

HENRICK

You have it as good as two adult people could possibly have it. You two are suited for each other. You both have interesting jobs, good finances and a beautiful home . . .

EVA

With a big garden . . .

MARGARETA

A big garden . . .

EVA

Where no children are playing.

ANN

(*to Henrick*) You sound so stupid. Are you that stupid?

EVA

But you get used to it. I wouldn't have had any time to spend with them anyway.

MARGARETA

If it had been that terribly important, you'd have had the possibility of adopting a child. You were supposed to go to Sri Lanka a couple of years ago, weren't you?

HENRICK

That was something you'd planned, right.

ANN

How lovely . . . to lease a little dark person out there in your fancy suburb.

HENRICK

Shut up! . . . Ann, dear . . .

EVA

Everything was set to go.

ANN

All the papers were in place. You were just waiting.

EVA

We'd sent five thousand to some woman down there.

ANN

And then you got your answer.

MARGARETA

Only five thousand?

EVA

Then they called and said that we could fly down there. We bought tickets, got our shots, bought baby things . . .

ANN

And I promised to be there when you came back . . . John and I would be there to meet you.

EVA

The same day we were leaving Mathias suddenly said: I don't want to go.

ANN

God, how awful.

EVA

I don't either, I said.

MARGARETA

What kind was it? Was it a boy?

EVA

Suddenly he felt that he couldn't do it, that it would be wrong to adopt a child just to show that we couldn't have one of our own.

MARGARETA

Was it a boy?

HENRICK

When was that?

EVA

No, it was a girl . . . That was the last time.

HENRICK

You never told us this before.

MARGARETA

You never told me this before!

EVA

I'm sorry.

MARGARETA

Why didn't you tell me about this?

HENRICK

Was it long ago?

EVA

No. (*calmly*) I don't tell you everything.

MARGARETA

So, suddenly he didn't want to?

EVA

No.

MARGARETA

What a bastard!

ANN

I can feel it; I hear it in your voices, the way you talk to each other. That there's nothing there . . . but no one talks about it while it's going on. You talk about it after a couple of months, when everything has been decided.

EVA

What?

ANN

That it's over. That you've decided to get a divorce.

EVA

Over? . . . Divorce?

HENRICK

They have not.

MARGARETA

It's not over!

ANN

Yes it is. Everything is so dead between you two, it's so buried.

MARGARETA

Oh Ann, you're so silly!

HENRICK

Is that what you'd like, Ann?

ANN

No, but there's nothing left. The bickering is over, the little confrontations are over – now everything has been put in a locked jar.

EVA

That doesn't sound very good.

ANN

It's a hell of a serious situation.

MARGARETA

Don't you have enough of your own problems? . . . Do you really believe that a marriage that's lasted for seventeen years just simply ends . . . without us noticing anything?

ANN

Apparently. You haven't even noticed that yours has ended.

HENRICK

What do you want us to do!

MARGARETA

It doesn't end like that!

HENRICK

What do you want from us?

ANN

Nothing. You know I'm right, but you don't have the guts to say anything. . . . You've understood everything, exactly, but you don't have the strength to . . .

MARGARETA

My God, Ann, you're so mean!

ANN

Yes.

MARGARETA

Is it these times we live in, that makes you so mean?

ANN

Yes, maybe it is.

MARGARETA

Couldn't you try to grow up a little, try to rise above your own . . . emotions?

ANN

No, I can't.

MARGARETA

For your own sake . . . poor Ann . . . poor little Ann.

ANN

(*to Eva*) She's like a bad actress. Not a single note that's real. . . . So, what's going to happen now?

EVA

I'll continue to live.

ANN

What? . . . You and Mathias?

EVA

I don't know. (*pause*) I don't know. . . . Mathias thinks we should learn how to sail.

ANN

Sail?

EVA

A boat. . . . That's his lifelong dream.

ANN

Do you want to learn how to sail?

EVA

No. (*pause*) I don't want to learn anything new. (*pause*) I want to continue with what I know. I don't want to learn new things.

MARGARETA

I get so sad . . .

ANN

You really shock me with what you say.

EVA

Yes, that's what Mathias says too.

ANN

The way you talk.

MARGARETA

(*to Eva*) Don't worry about what she says. You shouldn't care about that. She just wants everyone to feel as bad as she does.

HENRICK

(*to Ann*) Yes, we don't care about your hallucinations.

ANN

So, you don't care that Eva is dying.

MARGARETA

I can't take it when you're like this.

ANN

Me neither!

MARGARETA

Things aren't the way you say they are.

EVA

(*quietly*) No, nothing is what it seems . . . nothing is what it seems in this life.

MARGARETA

Eva is very stable. You really are.

HENRICK

Good common sense.

MARGARETA

Strong.

ANN

Like you.

MARGARETA

(*to Eva*) You aren't the kind of person who gives up easily. No, you aren't squandering your life away.

EVA

No, I hang in there to the bitter end, whatever happens.

ANN

(*politely*) Not like me, you mean? (*pause*) Hello, were you referring to me?

MARGARETA

Yes! Really! Like you! (A*nn laughs.*) You squander both people and things. You march on like a . . . a brutal terrorist! You can't even find a real job that'll provide you with a living wage even though you're almost forty years old. How many jobs have you had?

ANN

Eighty-five.

MARGARETA

You've worked for cultural institutions, in social services, in libraries and I don't know what . . . drama coach, art teacher, gallery assistant . . . and now you're a waitress in a pitiful restaurant. . . . It's unbelievable . . . all the money we've spent on her. . . . What's the use of your good education?

ANN

You can go to hell! Bitch!

MARGARETA

That's not very nice.

ANN

(*to Henrick*) Can't you get her to shut up?

MARGARETA

(*to Henrick*) I think she needs a good, strong reprimand. Why not a slap in her face? Why not thirty years ago?

ANN

You're fucking crazy!

HENRICK

This is getting worse than ever . . .

EVA

I think I should leave.

MARGARETA

No, my friend, you have to stay. You never know what might happen.

ANN

You haven't put one cent into my education, not one cent! I've paid for everything myself, and for the next fifty years I'll have to pay the government back. Believe me, I never got one fucking penny from you for my education!

MARGARETA

Education to become what . . . ha, ha, ha!

ANN

Not a fucking penny! Don't lie!

MARGARETA

What was it you were studying to become?

ANN

None of your fucking business!

MARGARETA

Was it a psychologist . . . Or a philosopher?

ANN

None of your damn business!

MARGARETA

Philosopher! You! Ha, ha, ha!

HENRICK

I wonder what our neighbors are thinking.

ANN

I had to work overtime as a waitress to pay for my studies! So, take that back! (*screams*) Take it back!

HENRICK

Stop the shouting, both of you!

MARGARETA

Not to mention your three or four abortions with totally different men!

HENRICK

Please lower your voice!

MARGARETA

Me? I'm supposed to lower my voice?

ANN

Take it back!

MARGARETA

No, I will not. I won't even take one word back. This is my home, this is my husband, and you are my children. You all better behave properly in my home.

ANN

Just stay out of my abortions! (*Henrick leaves*) The abortions are mine! I had them, not you—you don't know anything! I was with the same man for twelve years! For twelve years! That's not enough for you!

MARGARETA

(*almost hysterical*) I've been with Henrick for forty-four years! For forty-four years!

ANN

Because you tied him up, you chained him to you as tightly as you possibly could!

HENRICK

(*comes back*) I beg you . . .

ANN

You're an expert at chaining people, but you can't tie me down any longer! I'm free!

HENRICK

Ann! That's enough!

MARGARETA

As far as I remember your biggest problem as a child was your tooth-retainer.

HENRICK

This is too much. I can't take it anymore.

MARGARETA

And we sure know what you do when things get to be too much for you.

HENRICK

I'm leaving.

MARGARETA

You leave.

ANN

That's not possible. I've tried that since I was four or five.

MARGARETA

You really are tiresome. (*to Eva*) You don't say anything. You just sit there quietly. You don't feel part of all this, do you? You and I, we don't feel part of this. It's just words, words, words. (*takes Eva's hand*) You must not leave me.

EVA

No, no.

MARGARETA

Promise me that.

EVA

No, I won't leave you.

HENRICK

Why don't we try to do something else?

ANN

Yes, I guess that's all you can say!

MARGARETA

What? Clean up the kitchen, you mean?

HENRICK

It's late and I . . .

EVA

And you? (*pause*)

HENRICK

I get so . . . I get the feeling . . . that I don't know who I am any longer.

MARGARETA

No. (*stands up*) Me neither. (*about Ann*) I don't know who she is, and why she comes over here causing problems all the time.

ANN

(*to Henrick*) That's good, Dad. That's good!

HENRICK

What?

ANN

That you don't know who you are any longer.

HENRICK

I don't like it. It's unpleasant.

MARGARETA

Why don't you prescribe something calming for your unhappy daughter?

EVA

Demerol.

ANN

You've become a dog, dear dad.

MARGARETA

What are you supposed to do when you obviously don't enjoy each other anymore, but still feel a great responsibility?

ANN

Dad, I saw you in a store the other day, and I was shocked, you looked so fucking lost and confused, and I realized that your life is just an empty wreck. . . . There's no connection to anything on this earth any longer. I don't understand where you get the strength to get up every morning. You've hardly any patients left, your office looks awful, everything is filthy.

MARGARETA
It is not. I clean once a week . . . and Eva brings newspapers and magazines.

EVA
You brought your theater magazines and whatever else you had.

ANN
When I saw you in the store you looked so alone. You looked like an old animal that had been wounded, looking for a place to hide. When I see you starting to fall apart, it becomes enormous, so important . . . I get frightened.

MARGARETA
Oh, how touching. I'm sure everyone is as touched as I am. Is this a scene from your play?

ANN
Dad . . .

EVA
I guess you're allowed to be tired after a long day's work.

MARGARETA
Henrick's mother was also high-strung like Ann. She also wanted to write. . . . Maybe it's genetic.

ANN
Dad . . .

MARGARETA
Very beautiful, very, very intelligent, very gifted . . . and completely unreliable. She also had a hard time differentiating reality from fiction.

ANN
Dad . . .

MARGARETA

Finally they had to lock her up. She became totally insane.

ANN

Help me, Dad. Now it's my turn to get help.

MARGARETA

Why do you need help? You, who can manage everything so well; you, who know everything; you, who have all the answers—how to take care of children, how to care for a home—since you've read everything there is to read about psychiatry and psychology.

ANN

I don't feel well.

MARGARETA

No, I don't think you are well.

ANN

Dad . . .

HENRICK

Yes, yes . . . I'm here . . .

MARGARETA

Dear little Ann . . . let me tell you . . .

ANN

(*screams*)

MARGARETA

If you'd only listen. (*Ann screams*) That Henrick . . . (*Ann screams*) Henrick. Henrick . . . (*Ann screams, then silence. Margareta is about to say something, but Ann screams again.*) Hysteria. Pure hysteria. (*Ann screams, then silence. pause, very calmly*) Henrick was never able to make any decisions regarding you or me or our family, ever. He had others do it for him.

ANN

Yes, you made them.

MARGARETA

I must say, I don't understand how he can be a physician. . . . Yes, I did, I had to. I was the only one here. If you think that that was what I wanted, then you know as little about me as you know about everything else. Someone in the family, unfortunately, has to be the responsible one, the strong one, even if you aren't suited for it. I didn't particularly like it, but . . . I fell for Henrick, and I fell hard, and you two came rather quickly. Everything seemed bright. Not until later do you get to know one another. In the beginning you don't really want to see who the other one is, you aren't looking for his weaknesses, you try to remain a happy person as long as possible. (*pause*) This is the way it was, you see: Henrick had a mother . . . whom he never left, who never let him go. Henrick obeyed her in everything, he defended everything she did. In seconds his whole world could change if she said something negative. It became dark and cold and dangerous. Of course he knew that she was sick, but still, she had such incredible power over him. She spent ten years in a mental hospital, and I think Henrick visited her there at least four times a week, bringing candy and gifts. Of course it had an effect on our marriage. Finally I gave him an ultimatum. Like it says in the Bible: A man has to leave his father and his mother and be with his wife. He cried and begged, but I stood firm. It felt very strange to fight with a mother over her son. She never forgave me. Once a month we'd visit her together . . . she was terrible to me. Yes, excuse me, but . . . she could say the most horrible things . . . and there were sexual things too. She even tried to seduce him. She was something! She used every trick a woman and a mother has, and when that didn't work out for her she started to belittle and demean him . . . and I saw his shame and how he started to shrink away . . . how he died little by little . . . and then, for me to try to get him back, to build him up again . . . but there was always something inside him that I couldn't reach, something he couldn't give me, because it belonged to her. I never got . . . never . . . never . . . I felt an incredible longing . . . I was longing . . . he never could . . . I stopped trying, and I devoted my time to the two of you. I couldn't leave him . . . he was kind and polite, but I lost my joy for life. I couldn't stay at home. I wanted to get out . . . wanted to work . . . and then it ended in a catastrophe, one might say. . . . I suddenly met a man. It was rather serious. . . . Maybe I could've left then, if I'd been given a little push, I wanted to leave . . .

ANN

When was that?

MARGARETA

. . . but I didn't leave. . . . No one is there to forgive me for that. . . . I think that was the mistake of my life. . . . But I was so young, and so off-balance. . . . But the forbidden love brought something good with it—I didn't give a damn about Henrick and his mother any more. Henrick and I were married in the fall of 1943. Eva was born in June 1944. I met that man, I don't even remember what he looked like, in 1950. . . . A man . . . a boy . . . don't remember what he looked like. I started to work in the library right after Ann was born. Just a young man who came in to borrow some books. We liked the same kind of books; they became our connection, our messages . . .

ANN

Messages!

MARGARETA

. . . between us, secret messages about feelings . . . that grew—and finally made my fear go away. . . . Those were the happiest years of my life . . . and the unhappiest. It lasted for two years. Actually I was the one who took the initiative. He took out a collection of poems and I underlined a few words about longing . . .
            "My body, my whole being on fire.
            A fire that can't be extinguished,
            Will not be diminished . . ."
Then I waited for the moment when he'd bring the book back. Well . . . after that we met and went for long walks, we went to the movies and to restaurants. He had a rented room downtown. . . . He begged me to get a divorce, but I didn't dare. I guess I was too bourgeois. I had already decided, somewhere within me, what my life was supposed to be . . . under my skin . . . and also, Ann was so young . . .

ANN

Yes I was, young and smart!

MARGARETA

Then I noticed that Henrick had started to drink. Every evening after nine o'clock he began to drink and he drank until he was almost unconscious, but never a word, never a complaint or a reprimand. I realized he'd been drinking for quite some time. There were times I could follow his journey from the living room to his room. We slept in different rooms because I would find his clothing thrown on the floor. I didn't dislike Henrick, I've never disliked Henrick, but I couldn't do anything for him.

EVA

I didn't know any of this.

MARGARETA

Of course you didn't. No one knew. Eventually it died . . . in one way or another.

ANN

Did he know?

MARGARETA

Know what? About the other?

ANN

Dad.

MARGARETA

No, he didn't know anything about Henrick, except that I was married.

ANN

Dad, I mean. Did he know about the other man?

MARGARETA

No, not at the time. He didn't know anything. He doesn't really notice much.

ANN

Of course he did! There's no one who doesn't know when the other one has started a new relationship.

MARGARETA

He already had a relationship with his mother! That was enough for him!

ANN

There isn't anyone who doesn't know. Well, maybe two people on this earth.

EVA

And one of them is me.

MARGARETA

He wouldn't have reacted the way he did then, when I told him.

EVA

How?

MARGARETA

How? Well, he cried. He reacted as if he was totally surprised. He sat in bed and cried . . . and cried.

HENRICK

I'm the one you're talking about.

MARGARETA

Yes.

HENRICK

I'm sitting here. Maybe you haven't noticed?

MARGARETA

All this was so long ago.

HENRICK

Should I kill myself?

MARGARETA

No, why?

HENRICK

Or what do you want?

MARGARETA

I don't want anything. It's Ann! She has forced me to talk about all this! She forces everyone to talk about what they don't want to talk about.

HENRICK

I've tried to behave as civilly as I possibly can . . . but I don't want to be treated like an old animal, that you don't know what to do with. I don't want to get buried in your memories! (*extremely angry*) Why can't we continue our silence for twenty more years?

MARGARETA

Yes, why not?

ANN

Dad, it's only human to feel the way you feel!

MARGARETA

(*as if in present time*) If you weren't so dependent on your mother it wouldn't have happened! Then I wouldn't have had a need for him, someone to be close to and to love. I don't even remember what he looked like!

HENRICK

I don't remember what you look like.

MARGARETA

What kind of life is that! You marry a man who spends his evenings looking at photographs of his mother as a young woman!

HENRICK

That doesn't concern you. Don't denigrate my feelings.

MARGARETA

Who whispers her name over and over while his face is streaming down his tears. No, his tears are streaming down his face while life passes by . . . is sitting there thumbing through old photographs and letters from a sick woman . . .

HENRICK

Those were poems!

MARGARETA

While life is pulsating out there . . .

HENRICK

Those are wonderful poems, great poems.

MARGARETA

Street cars and buses honking . . . happy, young people looking for fun
and enjoyment. . . . What kind of life have we had? What kind of life?

HENRICK

She was incredibly gifted.

MARGARETA

How? She was dangerous . . . I didn't dare to let her visit when the girls
were small.

HENRICK

If she'd been met with some kind of understanding . . . if someone had
supported her, a young sensitive woman who suddenly had the
responsibility of a small child . . .

MARGARETA

One small child! My mother cared for three children and all of us have
managed very well!

HENRICK

Your parents were well off . . . they were both professors. My mother
lived all alone in a small village in Lapland.

MARGARETA

She never took care of herself either, I mean her appearance.

HENRICK

(*to Ann*) That's not true. You would've understood her, you would've
seen her for who she was.

MARGARETA

Oh yes, you could really see her . . . she stood out . . . dressed in rags,
used to go looking for garbage and had hardly any furniture, and she
pushed herself on people!

HENRICK

(*to Ann*) There are those of us who can't experience other people's
sensitivity. There are those with no talent for music, and those who lack
a sense of humor. You can't blame them for it. That's just the way it is.

MARGARETA

I found it very hard, very difficult, to find anything to laugh about in a human being who consciously tries to destroy other people's lives and homes . . .

HENRICK

I was the only one . . . only I could take care of her. I couldn't just leave her to herself.

MARGARETA

Sons usually have to leave their mothers, at least after they've met their wives. You still sit here taking care of her, and you don't see the needs of the people around you.

HENRICK

I couldn't . . .

MARGARETA

No, you couldn't do anything.

HENRICK

I couldn't just run away and leave her all alone and confused among strangers in a mental hospital.

MARGARETA

So instead you left me all alone with a small child.

HENRICK

You managed very well, she was sick.

MARGARETA

Sick! When did she get sick? When she didn't get her way, when the whole world wouldn't bend according to her needs. . . . She couldn't write that "great Swedish novel," only talk about it! She didn't have enough talent . . . just confused ideas, or whatever. She was so kind in the beginning and thought it was nice that a woman had come into Henrick's life. . . . There was nothing strange about her the first year, except that she talked incessantly and never listened to anyone, just like Ann . . . but really crazy. That didn't happen until you told her that you were going to marry me. Then she got really sick. . . . She kept calling me every day and told me nasty things behind your back. . . . She tried to

make me think that you were weak and helpless and lazy . . . not a real
man. . . . But when I didn't answer her the way she'd expected me to . . .
I said that everything was just fine . . . then she started to say horrible
things about me. . . . She has been here like a terrible ghost for almost
forty years. . . . We've had her here the whole time . . . inside of you, in
your thoughts and in your guilt. . . . She has sucked out your strength and
your . . . well, your feelings for this family. . . . I guess she won. . . . You
treat Ann the same way you treated her. . . . You bend, you tolerate all
the horrible things she says about me. . . . She's your mother reincarnate.

ANN
I knew it would come back to me sooner or later.

MARGARETA
. . . and then you apologize to her, because I had to teach her what was
right or wrong . . . who the mother is in this house, and who's the
daughter! You don't have to be a psychologist to understand how
confusing it must be for a child when the father doesn't know if she's his
daughter or his mother! And, as she said, which is absolutely correct . . .
you aren't a real father, you're just pretending. . . . Children know that
immediately.

ANN
Well, maybe now you'll give me a chance to say something . . . for a
change.

MARGARETA
You've talked all night. That's enough.

ANN
(*very calmly, slowly*) That's . . . not what I remember . . . and I'd guess
that I'm just as authentic a witness as you are.

EVA
Dad is talking now.

ANN
He is?

MARGARETA
I don't hear anything.

EVA

Weren't you going to say something?

HENRICK

No . . . what good would that do?

ANN

Yes, well . . . anyway . . . my strongest memories . . . were that she was after me too . . . because he liked me too much.

MARGARETA

He's sitting here . . . as he himself says.

EVA

Is he really?

MARGARETA

Strange, how easy it is to talk about you in the past tense while you're present. You got that from your mother. Your mother always did.

ANN

I mean that it's clear that we were rivals. . . . It sounds so innocent, but it wasn't.

MARGARETA

Yes, I'm obviously past tense as well. We're both past tense, Henrick. Isn't that nice?

ANN

That I was the rival? . . . Mother's rival for Dad? Wasn't that how it was?

MARGARETA

Don't ask Dad that question.

ANN

Dad?

MARGARETA

He's a man . . .

ANN

Dad!

MARGARETA
. . . or at least he has manly characteristics. Men feel flattered by female attention, especially from daughters, who don't see them for what they are.

ANN
He thought it was more fun to talk to me than to you. I loved to talk to him and be with him. He didn't lie. I remember once when I was very unhappy because I had to go to that terrible nursery school, where I didn't want to be, because I thought I looked ugly and strange. Suddenly he brought me to the mirror in our hallway and said: "Look at you, don't you see what a wonderful little girl you are? Look at your beautiful eyes and your lovely hair. You're kind and wise and full of wit." So I looked at myself and I saw that it was true . . . and I stopped crying.

MARGARETA
That sounds very nice. . . . However, I was the one who read to you when you were sick. Not Dad.

ANN
Thank you.

MARGARETA
I liked doing it. Dad was in the living room . . .

HENRICK
Where was that?

EVA
Here, where we're sitting now. Same room.

MARGARETA
Very often he'd spend evenings at his office, staying quite late. . . . I'd get so worried that he'd suddenly behave the way he did at home. Lose all discipline.

ANN
So, you read to me?

EVA
I remember that too.

ANN

What did you read?

MARGARETA

Mein Kampf, obviously. No, *Tom Sawyer*.

ANN

Tom Sawyer?

MARGARETA

Yes, the book.

ANN

Tom Sawyer . . . did I like it?

MARGARETA

Outside it was snowing, and I felt happy and peaceful. You were afraid of the sound of the elevator when it was on its way up.

ANN

Did I like *Tom Sawyer*?

MARGARETA

I don't know whom you were afraid of. Yes, you really did. I liked reading to you.

ANN

I guess you liked listening to your own voice.

MARGARETA

Ya, ya . . . it felt so peaceful.

EVA

I remember how happy I felt when Dad came home. I ran out to the entrance to be the first one at the door.

ANN

Yes, we used to compete as to who could get into Dad's arms first. You always won, because you pushed me away.

EVA

I did not.

                                   ANN
Yes, you did.

                                   EVA
No, I didn't.

                                   ANN
Yes, you did!

                                   EVA
No, I'm telling you, I never did things like that. I never pushed anyone.

                                   ANN
Oh yes you did, I don't know how many times you pushed me and I fell
to the floor and hurt myself.

                                   EVA
I guess I ran faster than you, because I was older and had longer legs.

                                   ANN
That you used to kick me with, yes. I could hear him when he opened the
downstairs door and when it closed and when he opened the elevator
door. . . . Then I couldn't help calling out: "Daddy is here, Daddy is
here."

                               MARGARETA
Yes, you really were Daddy's little girl, all the way.

                                   EVA
I also heard him coming, but I wasn't stupid enough to announce it.

                                   ANN
Anyway, it always ended with you pushing me down or pulling my hair.
I hated that.

                                   EVA
I guess I wanted to be first for a change.

                                   ANN
You didn't have to be so mean. . . . I was just happy.

MARGARETA

I'd think most kids get happy when a dad comes home.

EVA

Nothing to fight about anyway.

ANN

Well, still, that's the way it was! After that I sat in his lap the whole evening.

MARGARETA

After you'd pushed Eva down, yes.

ANN

You mean, after I'd pushed you down.

MARGARETA

If you've grown up harboring the idea that you've pushed your own mother away from her husband, your father, I've got to say that you have a rather sick understanding of how our roles were played out in this family.

ANN

That's right! That's exactly what I've been trying to tell you all night long! I've got a sick understanding of who was what! Where does it come from? I didn't make it up, it was inflicted on me!

EVA

My God . . . now you've got to stop.

MARGARETA

This time I thought we were talking rather calmly about things, anyway.

ANN

Why should I stop? Since I've never been told the truth.

MARGARETA

I don't think there is one truth . . . we've all our own truths.

ANN

But you've stolen mine . . . everything I say you say is wrong!

EVA

You've got one version and Mom has another one. Couldn't you be satisfied with that?

MARGARETA

Yes, I could.

ANN

Everything about me is wrong!

EVA

So, what do you want then?

ANN

What I want?

MARGARETA

Yes?

EVA

What do you want?

ANN

I want . . . I want . . . I want so much.

MARGARETA

For me to die.

EVA

Mom, please, let Ann talk now.

ANN

May Ann talk now? Is she allowed to talk now?

MARGARETA

All right, now tell us what you really want . . . so that the family may consider it. Finally.

ANN

I want you to keep quiet. Once and for all.

MARGARETA

But I'm not allowed.

EVA

Mom.

MARGARETA

Yes, I'll be quiet.

(*pause*)

EVA

What are you waiting for?

ANN

Now I've nothing more to say. . . . Yes, I do, but I'll wait . . .

EVA

For what?

ANN

For Dad.

MARGARETA

For Henrick? Yes, he's been sitting here quiet for so long . . . that we forgot about him again.

ANN

I'm never going to forget him.

EVA

Dad.

ANN

Yes, Dad.

EVA

Did you hear that?

HENRICK

Yes, I hear everything.

                              EVA

Ann wants you to say something?

                          MARGARETA

Is this some kind of group therapy? Then I don't want any part of it.

                              EVA

You are part of it.

                            HENRICK

I've been silent for forty years.

                              ANN

That sounds terrible. I mean it sounds terrible that it seems so natural . . .
so true.

                            HENRICK

Yes, but what's there to say?

                              ANN

Tell us HOW IT WAS!

                            HENRICK

Yes, but that's what we've been talking about all night.

                              ANN

WHAT HAPPENED? . . . Why are you all out to get me?

                          MARGARETA

No one is.

                              EVA

Only you, yourself, Ann.

                              ANN

Why are you like this . . . Dad?

                            HENRICK

I guess I'm like most people of my generation.

                              ANN

Like dead, Dad . . . so dead, dead. . . . Why are you so dead?

HENRICK

I'm not dead!

MARGARETA

Me neither.

EVA

No one's dead.

ANN

I'm dead . . . but I still hurt.

(*pause*)

HENRICK

What do you want me to say?

ANN

I want you to be alive, naked . . .

MARGARETA

If you want Dad to start to undress . . .

HENRICK

It's too late.

ANN

What's too late?

HENRICK

It's too late to go back again . . . to us . . . whomever we were. To my mother, to those places, where we were young, where it meant something. . . . One has to live an orderly life.

MARGARETA

In my memory you're just like some coil of smoke . . . in some street, in some room . . .

HENRICK

I don't remember anything.

MARGARETA

Still, we're in the same apartment, we're exactly the same people—I mean almost nothing has changed . . . except now our daughters can come with accusations . . .

HENRICK

Anyway, it's finished, over. If ever there was something that happened. I rather think that the fact that nothing happened might be the worst of it.

MARGARETA

But it isn't over. Look at Ann, how she's crying and screaming and carrying on. You never participate in our problems or our happiness, what little happiness we've got . . .

ANN

Meaning Eva.

MARGARETA

You've stayed high up above it all. (*to Ann*) Stop the competition for God's sake! (*to Henrick*) I never know what you're feeling. You always wear your mask however much you're provoked. I never know if there's someone in there . . . who's alive, who's hurting, who feels and wants something?

HENRICK

Do you want me to hit you, speak loudly and be vulgar, fall down and throw books and china at you?

MARGARETA

Yes, yes, yes . . . I wouldn't mind that at all.

ANN

Don't you ever feel like doing that?

HENRICK

No. Sorry, I don't. I'd just feel very silly.

MARGARETA

Not half as silly as you are now, sitting here as a . . . passenger. Stand tall, stand up from your grave, your sorrows or whatever it is that you carry with you. . . . You can't just continue like this . . . but it demands some tough action . . . some, what's it called . . . balls, to use a rather unpleasant expression. Some manly behavior. . . . I'm talking about manly determination and strength and some hell raising . . . that doesn't have to take the shape of brutality . . .

EVA

We know what you mean.

ANN

How can you be so terrible?

EVA

So, why did you ever marry him?

MARGARETA

Terrible? I've had to constantly build Henrick up, with some help from you, Ann, now and then. It's been like trying to steady a giant. I've had to run around like the little people in *Gulliver's Travels* to keep him on his feet . . . and then when I got him to stand up—well, now I'm exaggerating a little—I was so worn out that I didn't know why I did it.

EVA

Why did you marry him then?

MARGARETA

Because I . . . well, why do you get married? . . . Because I thought he was the man I was in love with, of course! I guess I didn't want to see who he really was deep inside.

ANN

So, that's why you dislike him so much?

MARGARETA

No, no, no . . . I've never disliked Henrick. Never, never . . . no, I've . . .

ANN

Despised him?

MARGARETA

No, not that either. I'm not a person who despises.

EVA

What is it then that you've been feeling?

ANN

If you've had any kind of feelings.

MARGARETA

I hate the word—feeling. I've taken care of a home and two children. I've done a good job. Every morning I've been at my work, well dressed and looking good . . . and what I've felt . . . well, that's of no concern to you, and I wouldn't tell you anyway! (*pause*) I've made peace with my very ordinary fate.

ANN

Yes, of course, now I remember.

HENRICK

(*to Margareta*) Do you know what you're saying?

MARGARETA

Yes, I do, I do . . . (*short pause*) I do. . . . I'm not bitter, in spite of everything we've had a good life.

HENRICK

It sounds like a shadow of a life . . . nothing more. Why us?

ANN

I remember all the silly jokes about Dad—and I remember that trip to Venice, when we were small . . .

EVA

It was Florence.

ANN

What's the difference.

EVA

It was Florence. It was wonderful.

ANN

If there are gondolas in Florence, then someone has been lying to me big time. Look at the picture where Mom is flirting with a young, greasy ice-cream vendor by the canal. It's in the photo album. Mom is almost inside his pants.

MARGARETA

But, my God . . .

ANN

Dad even took that picture!

MARGARETA

Well, you know about the Italians . . .

ANN

Pure pornography . . . He's almost pulling at your tits.

MARGARETA

Oh my, oh my . . .

ANN

(*to Henrick*) Didn't you see that? You took the picture?

MARGARETA

I'm leaving . . .

EVA

Dad.

ANN

Dad.

EVA

Aren't you going to say something?

ANN

Defend yourself?

HENRICK

Defend myself?

MARGARETA

Yes, defend yourself against something she thinks happened thirty years ago!

HENRICK

What do I have to defend myself against?

MARGARETA

The assaults on your manliness.

HENRICK

My manliness manages just fine.

MARGARETA

(*with irony*)Your three women turn on you like the goddesses of revenge. So, now my friend, you're in trouble.

ANN

I'm not out for revenge. I only want to understand. I want to know who you are. I've known who she is for a long, long time.

HENRICK

I am . . . like this.

ANN

After that everything could work out.

MARGARETA

Do you really believe that?

ANN

No, but there's a chance.

HENRICK

Well, I'm really the one you see sitting here. What should I say about myself? I guess the most important thing is what you do, how you act in life. . . . We walk around on this planet and we don't know anything. We try to become better people. You either have something to live for or you don't; if not, this is a life without worth. I think I can say that I'm quite calm, even harmonious, I'd say. I've never really had very strong emotions. If I did, I put them aside. (*pause*) I've cared for my work. . . . I've never doubted Margareta's feelings for me, however she's behaved. People express themselves differently. I have my own way. I love you . . . all three of you . . . as much as I'm capable of. . . . I'm not spending my whole time thinking about it . . . but I don't know that you can measure the strength of your feelings. . . . Hopefully you should complement one another. . . . You can love in different ways. I don't believe too much in words . . . words . . . those are to me like an empty apartment filled with old furniture. . . . You don't need that many words either, to say something important. That much I know from experience in my practice, when I have to deliver a serious message.

MARGARETA

There wasn't ever a serious message delivered in that practice.

HENRICK

I think it's the manner in which it's said that's important. . . . The words you need, they just come. . . . If I've had one emotion that has followed me my whole life, it would be . . . well, a feeling of sorrow, maybe . . . that I couldn't talk about. Not unhappiness . . . or worries . . . no, sorrow . . . regarding how what's beautiful is destroyed, how what's good is decimated.

EVA

What's that?

HENRICK

Yes, everything that . . . Mother . . . it went so fast. I wasn't prepared for it. We were happy. We belonged together, and then everything disappeared. You know what it looks like when an eight-millimeter film is about to end. It gets lighter and lighter, and people are seen as streaks, until suddenly everything becomes white, and then you wonder . . . what did they do after that? Who was that dark-haired, laughing woman, who used to visit us?

MARGARETA

I guess that was me.

HENRICK

No, you I can place.

MARGARETA

If she was wearing a big, dirty cap, then it was your mother.

ANN

Then what?

HENRICK

After that? No, there's nothing after that. Then is now.

ANN

Dad . . . I love you.

HENRICK

That's good. That's good. Thank you.

EVA

Me too.

HENRICK

I know, I know.

EVA

Mom too.

ANN

Yes, good, good that we love each other.

MARGARETA

Yes, I guess we have to.

ANN

Does it make you happy?

HENRICK

It's possible that I drank a tad too much . . . but it wasn't because I wanted to escape, but rather to force myself to keep . . . order . . . to keep stability in my existence . . . in order not to go under. I saw what happened to my mother, even though it wasn't as horrible as you tell it, you always exaggerate everything. It's a rather horrible experience to witness your own mother go insane, and not be able to help her in any way. Sometimes she would be as sharp as could be, and then suddenly she could say something . . . something from another world. I had to be there to tell her things that could help her, or just hold her in my arms. I had never learned anything about mental illness in my studies. I only remember books and lecture halls and how I used to assist at post mortem sessions. I remember that once I rented a skeleton, and I was on the bus going home, when the package opened up and the skeleton fell

on the floor, and people started to scream. . . . I think that was the
funniest thing that happened to me for seven years, otherwise it was like
military basic training. I rented two small, cold rooms. . . . I worked at
the hospital, I met Margareta, she was a student, mother got sick . . . and
I felt I had to choose between her and Margareta . . . and I chose you.
Everything about mother wasn't just about her illness. She was gifted.
Like Ann . . . alive, funny and sensitive—she was like a thin flame, filled
with life.

MARGARETA

That burned everything up.

HENRICK

A sensitive flame.

MARGARETA

I have to say, it's not always easy to have a sensitive flame as your rival.
Children have to be reared, be taught right from wrong, their daily home-
work. . . . They have piano lessons, ballet lessons, their hair has to be
braided. . . . Then you have your work to take care of, where you have to
be nice and helpful, and you have a husband who's really never present,
who you try to keep your marriage going with, and then you've got to be
a thin sensitive flame as well. You really do get frustrated when
unreasonable demands are put on you.

ANN

Yes, that's the way it is for me too.

MARGARETA

It is?

ANN

Yes, it is.

MARGARETA

The way it was for me?

ANN

Yes, most of the time. I'm both you and Grandma. I have to take care of
John, provide for us, and make sure that he's doing what he wants to do.

Then I also have to find time to express myself artistically. There's no one there to help me either.

MARGARETA

Well, that's very hard. Very difficult.

EVA

Yes, this is a hard time for mothers.

ANN

But I'm not giving up. I'm determined to manage.

(*pause*)

EVA

Well, then, I guess everything is good then.

MARGARETA

As good as it can be.

HENRICK

What?

MARGARETA

(*to Eva*) What were you going to say?

EVA

Nothing.

MARGARETA

But I thought . . .

ANN

Yes . . .

EVA

Oh, no . . . no, just that I didn't know that much about Grandma, except that she was a little nuts, and that she had such strange eyes. I was as happy as everybody else.

ANN

That was enough for you.

EVA

My dad was a doctor. I had my own room. It was about clothes and guys and I wanted to travel. Yes, I'm happy anyway, in spite . . .

ANN

In spite of what?

EVA

Well, this thing I have.

ANN

What thing?

EVA

But I guess I can't blame my parents for that. That's something I have to live with. It's . . . like a grave.

ANN

Fill it up, fill it, fill it up with money! Sorry, sorry. I'm so sorry. I'm so stupid, so stupid. You know I didn't mean it . . . but you do fill it with . . . all kinds of things that aren't good.

EVA

I can't fill it with something . . . good.

ANN

Stuff that only makes it worse.

EVA

It's not possible to fill it with anything but what's supposed to be there. But since that's not possible . . .

ANN

Please forgive me anyway. I'm so sorry.

EVA

I can't just give up. . . . That's what they say, people who know. And that's that. And I'll never exactly know when the day arrives when it's too late to get pregnant. There won't be a remarkable sound of any kind, like when a harp string breaks or a church door slams shut—it'll just be another pleasant day in my life. . . . Or maybe I'm so dumb that I'm

sitting here feeling terrible about something that doesn't exist anymore.
Maybe when I haven't had my period for six months I'll be sure . . .
that's why there's still a ray of hope within me, and that's what's so
terrible. . . . I'll never change or develop, except perhaps in my work. . . .
That's good, I like my work. But not me, the person, same body, only
getting older and older—it hasn't given life to anything, there's only
emptiness in there, it's only me that I have to fill with something . . . with
money, as Ann says in her brutal way . . . or to find some pleasant
experiences. . . . I'm so tired of my body, I just want to get rid of it . . . I
want to forget about it, I don't want it! What do I want it for, what good
does it do me?

MARGARETA

My dearest, my dearest . . . (*Margareta has gotten up and walked over to
Eva and is hugging her.*) Oh, you can't talk like that, not like . . .

EVA

I hate it! I hate you!

MARGARETA

Not like that, not like that . . . my little Eva, my little child . . .

EVA

I hate you, I hate you!

MARGARETA

No, my dear, you don't hate me, you don't hate me. You don't hate your
body.

ANN

Let her express her feelings!

EVA

I feel calm. I feel terribly calm. (*pause*) I just get so goddamn angry
when I run into problems everywhere, that could be so easily solved with
some good planning! That's all.

MARGARETA

Yes, yes, I know.

EVA

This can't be solved, no one can solve it! It's an illness, that destroys everything, and you don't even notice. They say that you dry up, you get hard and cold and strange. . . . You don't get hard, you get like the edges of a wound that never heals. No one understands that.

ANN

What about Mathias?

MARGARETA

He's a man. That's not the same thing.

EVA

I could've killed him . . .

HENRICK

Eva, don't talk . . .

EVA

Yes, I could have. If it had helped in any way. (*pause*) Right now all we can do is say bad things about each other in other people's presence. (*pause*) We don't talk about this anymore. . . . We work on the premise that the possibilities are disappearing one by one. . . . It's not his fault, but it is his fault too, and mine . . . and I feel like throwing up. I'm terrified of a talk. I'd rather throw up than have that conversation again.

ANN

About what?

EVA

About what we should do. (*pause*) Otherwise I manage pretty well, at least I think so. I usually don't feel like this . . . like tonight. It hurts, but I guess that's good. . . . Of course it's always there, in my thoughts . . . but I can't walk around thinking about it constantly. I've got to find a way to live with it somehow.

MARGARETA

Sure, sure . . . of course you do.

EVA

Yes. Of course I do . . . in some way.

HENRICK

Do you mean that . . . that you're talking about a divorce?

EVA

No . . . yes, we always do . . . but no one has the courage to do something.

ANN

You can come to me. If you want to talk, I mean.

EVA

I don't want to talk about it anymore. I don't want to talk.

MARGARETA

No. No.

HENRICK

Let's not talk about it.

MARGARETA

Let's not talk about it anymore.

EVA

It's my life. (*pause*) I don't want it to be a topic for conversation. (*pause*) I want to go home.

HENRICK

We'll help you, if you need us.

MARGARETA

Yes. It's late.

HENRICK

Otherwise you can stay here, if you feel like it.

EVA

No, I don't feel anything.

MARGARETA

You're off tomorrow, right?

EVA

Today is Saturday, isn't it?

MARGARETA

That's right.

HENRICK

Yes. This has been a very strange evening.

MARGARETA

Yes, really . . .

ANN

Maybe this was the last time. Maybe it was the first time. . .

EVA

You're coming with me, aren't you?

ANN

. . . that we've talked to each other. . . . It's OK . . . John is with his daddy. He has a cold. I don't know what I'm doing. I'm thinking of going to Club Wasahof. Will you be going that way?

MARGARETA

Are you really going out to a club now? . . . Henrick?

ANN

I'm just going for a beer.

HENRICK

(*stands up*) Yes . . . I don't know what to say.

MARGARETA

Oh dear, you look so tired.

HENRICK

No, on the contrary . . . I feel . . . I feel uplifted somehow.

EVA

(*starts to put on her fur coat, her scarf, brushes her hair, turns around with a tired smile*) Well, back to being myself again. . . . What choice do I have? I want to thank you for this evening.

MARGARETA

Yes, I almost forgot what we had to eat.

EVA

(*kisses her mother's cheek, hugs her dad*) I don't know what to say.

HENRICK

You don't have to say anything.

MARGARETA

No.

EVA

No, I know. Everything will be fine. . . . Are you ready?

ANN

Yes, I just have to put on my boots. (*They all stand silently while she puts her boots on.*)

HENRICK

Just like when she was little.

EVA

OK. See you soon.

MARGARETA

Bye, bye.

HENRICK

Take it easy. Drive carefully. It's almost winter.

EVA

It isn't that cold yet.

HENRICK

It can get cold very suddenly.

ANN

Well, I guess I should say thank you and goodbye too.

MARGARETA

Yes, thank you, dear. Take care.

ANN

Yes, I will.

MARGARETA

Thank you for coming over.

ANN

Sure. Bye, Dad. (*pause*) Listen, don't look so sad. You've got your whole life ahead of you.

HENRICK

You're right. Run now.

ANN

OK.

MARGARETA

OK, dear. We'll talk soon.

EVA

Bye, then.

HENRICK

Bye, bye.

(*The girls leave. Henrick closes the door. Margareta goes into the living room. Henrick remains for a moment, turns to her and looks at her as she quickly goes out to the kitchen. He tidies up the hallway, then he turns out the lights.*)

THE END

Major Plays by Lars Norén

1979	ORESTES
1981	A TERRIBLE HAPPINESS
1981	MUNICH – ATHENS
1981	SMILES OF THE INFERNO
1982	NIGHT IS MOTHER TO THE DAY
1982	CHAOS IS THE NEIGHBOR OF GOD
1982	DEMONS
1983	THE LAST SUPPER
1984	CLAUDIO (MANTEGNA PORTOFOLIO)
1985	THE COMEDIANS
1986	FLOWERS OF OUR TIME
1987	HEBRIANA
1988	AUTUMN AND WINTER
1988	BOBBY FISCHER LIVES IN PASADENA
1988	AND GIVE US THE SHADOWS
1989	TRUTH OR DARE
1989	SUMMER
1990	LOVE MADE SIMPLE
1990	CHINNON
1991	THE LAST QUARTET
1991	LOST AND FOUND
1991	THE LEAVES IN VALLOMBROSA
1992	MOIRE DI –
1992	STERBLICH
1994	ROMANIANS
1994	BLOOD
1994	A KIND OF HADES
1994	THE CLINIC
1994	TRIO TO THE END OF THE WORLD
1997	PERSONKRETS 3:1
1998	SEVEN/THREE
1998	SHADOW BOYS
2000	NOVEMBER
2000	ACT
2000	COMING AND GOING
2002	QUIET WATERS

2003 DETAILS
2003 CHILL
2005 WAR
2006 TERMINAL
2007 ANNA POLITKOVSKIA
2010 ORESTIEN
2012 FRAGMENTE

Acknowledgements

Without the "nudging" of Jane Altschuler this book would not have seen the light of day. Thank you, Richard Altschuler, for your guidance throughout this process.

My deeply felt "thank you" to Bjorn Melander, Bo Corre, Ulrika Josephsson, Niclas Nagler, Maggan Petersson, Eleanor Reissa and Mina and Moni Yakim.

I am very grateful to many New York actors who participated in readings and workshops.

Most of all, my love and thanks to my husband, Len Gochman, who has never wavered in his support.

CPSIA information can be obtained at www.ICGtesting.com
Printed in the USA
BVOW071402170313

315675BV00002B/161/P